VL

INVITATION
TO A LYNCHING

"You're gonna let a mob of plow-pushers lynch a cowman?" Trago asked incredulously. "That's the trouble with this outfit. You gamble like farmers—a dime-limit game. What time is it?"

"We got about an hour," Cuff said. "But how can four of us...?"

"One of us," Trago said scornfully, toeing into the stirrup. "I wouldn't ride across the road with the likes of you. I'll get him out and put him on a horse—and when you hear about it, you'll know I did it alone!"

TRAGO
FRANK BONHAM

A BERKLEY BOOK
published by
BERKLEY PUBLISHING CORPORATION

TRAGO

A Berkley Book / published by arrangement with
the author

PRINTING HISTORY
Dell edition published 1962
Berkley edition / November 1979

ISBN: 0-425-03895-5

A BERKLEY BOOK ® TM 757,375

Printed in the United States of America

CHAPTER 1

September had beaten Oklahoma into dust, and sent winds to blow the dust away. In the crowded day-coach of the Rock Island train, clouds of pulverized earth and coal-smoke swirled through the open windows and doors. The car was thronged with homesteaders and their paraphernalia of children, baggage, parcels and hopes— hopes they shared with anyone who would listen.

Farrell had listened most of the way across the country, though his boots, and the Stetson resting on the luggage rack above his head, made it plain that he was not a homesteader. He was one of the ranchmen the homesteaders had come West to finish off. They had started the job in 'Eighty-nine, when most of the Indian lands were opened to settlement; and now, four years later, they were back to finish it by pre-empting the last free range in the country—the Cherokee Strip.

Farrell was coming back from Washington, where he had wasted four months trying to get concessions for the cattlemen—some corner for them to exist in. He had failed.

Sitting by the window, he squinted out across the sunburned prairie. The grasshopper-swarm of settlers had leveled and obliterated everything familiar. In four years, they had re-made the short-grass country into an image of themselves—dust-colored and hopeless. It was a country tamed and with a ring in its nose, but a country which could not live in captivity and was dying of despair—like one of the old chiefs who had fought to keep his tribal lands, and had gone to prison.

It had been a comely, rolling land before the gang-plows broke it up and the awkward machines of the boomer clanked across it, flattening it and seeding it to crops the soil would not support. Plum thickets had traced the creeks which wound toward the Arkansas; stands of cottonwood and elm had stood on the flatness in ponds of shadow. Now the trees had been cut for firewood, and where the grass had grown green and tough, impoverished fields of wheat and kaffir corn burned under the yellow sun. On the flat landscape, small sod houses stood in the shimmering distance—one house to each hundred and sixty acres, set more or less square with the original surveyors' corners.

And now again the roads and trains were choked with men and women coming from the cities to have a go at farming—a hundred thousand of them to scramble after the last free land the nation had to offer them.

The conductor worked through the car, climbing over children and luggage. "Osage next," he droned. There was a stir among the passengers. Farrell tapped the conductor's arm as he passed.

"How about those horses of mine?"

"Everything's been arranged. We'll put the car on the siding for you."

The man next to Farrell looked at him. He was a big Alabaman with dark hair going thin; a loner, hard to figure. In his black trousers and white shirt he looked more citified and prosperous than most of the homesteaders on the train.

"How far from the Strip is this Osage?" he asked.

"Fifteen miles. The next stop's right on the line, though. Rockland."

The man grinned. "What are you trying to do—scare me off? Maybe I don't want to be right on the line. Maybe I'd like a spot where there'll be less competition for claims. You getting off at Osage?"

Farrell reached up to the luggage rack for his hat. "Yep."

"How big a place is it?"

"It's a siding, a dugout and some shipping pens. The nearest town is Hogan, twelve miles north."

Farrell clambered over the man and braced himself on the rocking floor to pull on his coat. He was of more than average height, with a whippy build. He was darker than a settler, a little less dark than an Indian, and his face was square and hard, with narrow gray eyes and a wide mouth.

The other watched him. "You're going to Hogan?"

Farrell looked at him. The Alabaman's face was swarthy and pitted. He tried to decide what he did for a living. He might be an adventurer, a small farmer, a horse-trader. "I'm going to Hogan," he said patiently.

"Did I hear you say you've got some horses to sell?"

"No. You didn't."

The Alabaman grinned again. "But you have got horses. That's good. They must bring quite a price out here. I'm surprised you aren't selling them."

"They're already spoken for."

"That's too bad. You can't drive much of a bargain with the buyers, then, can you?" The Southerner's smile said he saw right through him.

Farrell lifted his suitcase from the luggage rack. "A bargain on horses like these would be about five hundred dollars."

The other man whistled. "If you'd said fifty dollars, I'd 'a' tried for one."

As he set down his suitcase, Farrell noticed that the pretty girl across the aisle, who had boarded the train in Indiana, was struggling to get her own bag from the luggage rack. He hesitated over helping her—she seemed to spend quite a bit of time reading some sort of religious tract, and might resent the familiarity—but finally he said, "Can I help with that?"

She looked around. Then she smiled and stepped aside. He lifted the suitcase down, finding it surprisingly heavy. He hefted it. "Books," she explained.

"You're a schoolteacher?"

"No. I teach, but not school."

She took a large tapestry bag from her seat and groped in it. She was a very attractive girl, with reddish-blond hair and fair skin on which there were a few soot-smudges. She looked somewhat windblown and flushed with the heat.

"Is there a stage from Osage to Hogan?" she asked.

Farrell nodded. "It'll be there to meet the train."

The girl took a small kit from the tapestry bag, left the bag on the seat, and went forward to freshen up. Farrell carried her suitcase with his own back to the vestibule. When he returned for the rest of his things, the Alabaman was standing in the aisle. With his coat on, his shoulders looked bigger and more square. From the luggage rack he lifted a tin suitcase reinforced with a leather belt. He set a wide-brimmed black hat on his balding head and winked at Farrell.

"If this here Osage is good enough for you two, it's good enough for me."

Farrell shrugged. He had no desire to become any closer with this man, who was unmistakably a boomer—one of the men who would be out cutting up the pie which had belonged to the Indians and the stockmen until recently. But now the man offered his hand.

"My name's Johnson."

"Farrell."

"Wish you'd sell me one of those horses, friend. I'm going to be needing one."

An idea struck Farrell. He looked Johnson over. "They're not for sale. I'll tell you what, though. Can you ride in those clothes?"

"Sure."

"I'll pay you five dollars to ride one of my horses to Hogan. I've got a man in the car with them, but the two of us may have our hands full trailing them to town."

Johnson pursed his lips. His jaws were wide and strong, his eyes wide-set, black and cold. "So would three of us."

"I've got chain hobbles for them."

The girl was coming back down the aisle, picking a delicate path among children playing on the floor and parcels which cluttered the aisle.

"Okay," Johnson said. He peered up the aisle past the girl. "I've got a rebate coming on my ticket. Back in a minute, feller."

Feller. Johnson moved in fast. Vern Farrell watched him struggle past the blond girl, begging her pardon in a courtly manner and not forgetting to raise his hat, and pass out of sight in the vestibule. Farrell and the girl walked to the rear. Just as they reached it, a muted hoot of the train-whistle floated back to them, and with a sudden lurch the train began to slow. On the clattering iron floor, the dust boiling up around their feet, they faced each other. She had brushed the dust out of her hair and washed the specks of soot from her face.

"Thank you for carrying my bag out," she said, with a small, engaging smile. "People seem to be very helpful here in the Indian country." Though she read tracts, there was a lot of vitality about her. Farrell saw it in the expressive mouth and the warm sheen of her skin. She offered her hand.

"I'm Rachel Grant," she said.

"Vernon Farrell—a pleasure, miss."

"You're a rancher?"

"I used to be, until they closed the Cherokee Outlet to grazing—what they call the 'Strip' these days."

"What are you now?"

Farrell squinted at her. "Promise not to laugh?"

"Try me."

"I'm a Congressman."

"A Congressman! No," the girl laughed, "I don't believe you."

"I'm Delegate Farrell, from the Territory of Oklahoma. Or will be for a few more months. I was appointed to fill out the term of a man who died."

"And what did you do in Washington?" asked the girl with a twinkle of amusement, still not sure whether he was joking.

"Practically nothing. I was supposed to get some concessions for my constituents—the cow-crowd, that is. We wanted part of the Strip set aside for grazing. It was going to be called the Territory of Cimarron."

Rachel shook her head soberly. "Not a very popular idea right now."

"Very *unpopular*. I poured a lot of drinks, but I didn't get much accomplished. I'm almost afraid to go home."

There was a carborundum grinding of brake-shoes under their feet. A stack of creosoted ties flashed past, a mound of gravel.

"I'm sure your friends will understand," the girl said. "Besides, I heard you and the conductor talking about a carload of horses you've brought back with you. That doesn't sound as though you'd given up the fight."

Farrell smiled. "Are you a homesteader, by any chance?"

"No . . . not exactly." The girl slowly shook her head.

"Not exactly a teacher, not exactly a homesteader. You must be a gambler, then. That's about the only other type that comes to Oklahoma."

Rachel's eyes sparkled. "A gambler—perhaps that comes as close as anything. . . ."

Johnson came lurching back with his tin suitcase. The train stopped with a weary creaking of wood and steel and a great sigh of steam. He ducked his head to peer outside. "Oklahoma, eh? Don't look like much."

Farrell looked out at the fields beyond the litter of the station. Everything looked dun-colored and beaten

Jown. He could scarcely picture the way it had looked four years ago. "That's a fact " he sighed. "And it's going to look like less, after the Strip is opened."

CHAPTER 2

At Osage there was a yellow railway station at the foot of a long, lion-colored swale. A hundred feet from the tracks was a dugout with a log front, pressed back into the slope so that it was half cave. On a board over the entrance was the word:

MCGREW'S

McGrew, who sold liquor and a few provisions, was a rheumatic, scowling old man who had gone broke on a farm after the run of 'Eighty-nine. Behind the store were corrals where stage teams were kept. Two Indian hostlers were currying the horses which would take the stage back to Hogan after it came in.

Farrell, the girl and Johnson stood beside the tracks while a porter handed down their bags. Up and down the train other passengers were disembarking, some to transfer to the Hogan stage, others merely to stretch their legs. Rachel Grant shaded her eyes to gaze at McGrew's store. Then her glance ran up the long slope and turned north across the prairie. The panorama was blinding—sun on earth, sun on wheat-stubble. The sky itself was nearly as yellow as the sun.

"It's bleak," she said faintly.

Farrell nodded. "The trouble is, you're coming in late. The best part of the show's already over."

"What *was* the best part?"

"Before the boomers came."

"I bet that's us he's talkin' about," Johnson said. "All a cattleman wants is Oklahoma for a range and Kansas for a buck-pasture."

Farrell looked at him, first hard, then with a grin. "You aren't getting any closer to that horse, Alabama," he said. "Why don't you take the lady over to the store and buy her a sarsaparilla, while I check with my wrangler?"

Johnson offered Rachel Grant his arm. She did not take it. But she said agreeably, "I think that would be nice. It *is* a store—it's not a saloon, is it?"

"McGrew calls it a store."

They joined the other passengers walking toward it.

In the shade of the little railroad station, Farrell removed his coat and tie. He unwrapped the paper parcel he carried. It contained work-clothing, shaving things, and a pair of spurs. He put on the spurs and a denim jacket, and wrapped his town-coat and tie in the newspaper. Except for the trousers, now, he looked like any other working cowboy. He felt better. He had been made an ass of in the Capitol. Never again: people ought to do the things they were fitted for, he had learned.

He walked down the tracks toward the cattle-car and caboose. Couplings crashed and the train crew started the process of separating his car from the others. A small man in a white shirt and old denim pants was riding the catwalk of the car as it coasted backward onto the siding. The sun was mercilessly hot. The horses would need a lot of water traveling to Hogan. He hoped the homesteaders had not fenced off all the creeks and springs along the way.

Perhaps a more experienced man would have accomplished more in Washington, he thought, frowning to himself. He doubted it. The pressure of all those hundreds of thousands of landless people and railroad men standing behind their powerful lobbyists and Western Congressmen was too great for a group like his own—a few dozen cattlemen and some visionary Indian rights advocates.

Still, he had gained a concession or two, and he had a plan to suggest to the Cattlemen's Association members who had helped get him appointed as delegate. *By God, I'd better have!* he thought with grim humor. Tom Trago, who used to graze about half the Cherokee Strip, would be after his hide. Trago, almost a kinsman of Farrell's, had wanted to make a different kind of fight against the homesteaders—night-riding, haystack-burning—until the raids and the climate drove them out. But he had been voted down by the more conservative members.

But, being Trago, he had set out to make his own fight against the men he hated—the red-necked, humble destroyers of the soil, the graze, the game. He had burned a few barns, set the torch to some cornfields—and had had a horse shot out from under him one night by one of the deputy marshals who had recently been organized to control lawlessness in the Territory.

Trago had spent six months in a Federal prison. He would have been out about two months, now. It was impossible to conceive of all that arrogance and big-country strength compressed into one small jail cell. Farrell had heard from Old Man Cuff, another Association rancher, that Trago was free. But what was left? What had imprisonment done to him—broken him like an Indian bowl, or simply distilled the acid of his being to a pure, refined hatred? He would know before long.

He heard the stage-horn blare and saw the coach swinging down the road in a nutmeg cloud of dust. He stopped beside the car, where his puncher was now standing on the coupling gazing in at the horses. His name was Bill Spence, a warped and pallid little man who carried one shoulder high. Farrell had hired him at the stockyards where he bought the horses. At first he had thought the man was just out of the hospital, but it developed he was merely drying out after a prolonged drunk. He looked better now than he had looked in Kansas City. At some station he had managed to shave; there were bits of tissue over half a dozen cuts on his face, and he looked strained and convalescent.

"How are the horses looking?" Farrell asked him.

"Do with some grain before they go to work."

"They go to work in five days. How are *you* doing?"

"Why, I reckon I'll make it," Spence said ruefully, adding: "Gonna be close, though."

"Why don't you hire on with me for a while?"

"Doin' what?"

"I'll need a hand with these horses."

Spence was as ugly a little man as he could remember, with knobby jaws, a broken nose, and sad black eyes. "Okay," he said.

"How about you and whisky? Can you stay off it?"

Spence raised his hand. "I'm done, Mister Farrell! Me and whisky are all finished."

Finished until next time, Farrell thought. "Good for you." He smiled. "Get a little water in the horses while I get the hobbles. We'll trail them to Hogan this afternoon."

When he entered McGrew's place, six passengers transferring for Hogan were drinking sarsaparilla from stone bottles. It was a big, cool room with an earth floor littered with sacks of merchandise with their tops rolled down like stockings. The ceiling was low and supported by cottonwood poles. Behind the dry-goods counter, old McGrew was setting out the drinks from a washtub of cool water. Rachel and Johnson were standing among sacks and barrels of supplies. Out of deference to the ladies, even the men were drinking warm sarsaparilla. Seeing Farrell enter, Rachel smiled. In that cluttered gloom, her freshness glowed like a cnadle. A young homesteader in overalls and a checkered shirt was asking McGrew how you went about taking a claim. McGrew, a squat old man who always smelled of liniment, went on uncapping bottles.

"Well, first you get a registration c'tificate. Then you make a run for a claim when the cannons go off. If you get one, then you go back and register the claim at a land office. Then you go broke like everybody else."

Johnson grinned at him. "Old walrus like you was bound to go broke."

"Now, you watch your mouth," McGrew warned, glaring.

"Anybody can have bad luck," said the young fellow in the overalls. He was so full of hope and belief in himself that it was pathetic, Farrell thought—if you had watched them go broke last time.

"What about a dairy farm—that ought to go, oughtn't it?" the homesteader said. "Say you took a claim along a creek, where you'd have good graze and plenty of water...."

"A creek-claim? You're dreaming," Farrell said.

The young boomer's long face reddened. "Somebody's got to get the good claims! That's the chance we're all takin'. But, all right, say a man *did* get one—"

"He wouldn't unless he had a race-horse. There's a hundred thousand other boomers lined up along the Kansas and Oklahoma borders, and only a quarter of them will get homesteads.—What's a good horse bring now, McGrew?" Farrell asked the storekeeper.

"Last price I heard was eight hundred dollars. This was for a wind-broke racehorse. Just good for a short run."

"Eight hundred!" echoed several people.

McGrew made change. "Good bicycle'll cost you a hundred and fifty."

"Why, that's criminal!" Rachel Grant said.

Farrell tried a little of the soft drink and set it down.

"Suppose you do have a fast horse. You still don't know where to head it. You may be pounding your stake in a claim that's already taken! The land was surveyed twenty years ago, and the monuments are all grassed over."

Johnson watched him carefully, a man who did a lot of speculating. "I'll bet you know where they are, though."

Farrell smiled. "I'll bet there's only two men besides me who do, too. I'm talking about this end of the Strip. I know, and a man named Tom Trago knows, because we ranched the Strip for years."

"Who's the third?"

"Daniel Hogan. He was one of the original surveyors. He's the screaming eagle of the boomers, now. He knows every acre of the Strip."

"Oh, I know Mr. Hogan!" the young fellow exclaimed. "The town's named after him. I heard him speak at a rally last month!"

"I'll bet you did," Farrell said drily. Hogan—publisher, one-time drunk, patron saint of the landless—was the big boomer who had brought the first horde here in 'Eighty-nine, and had now brought another swarm of them to finish dividing up the last reservation of the Five Civilized Tribes. "I suppose Hogan promised to lead you personally to a nice claim on a creek?"

"I wish he had," the young fellow said ruefully.

McGrew spoke, setting out another bottle. "If you wanted him to put you on a claim, you should'a stuck by him when he was thumping the tub in Congress to get the Strip opened. There's a gang of people who backed him that he's personally leading into the Strip."

"Doesn't sound very democratic." Farrell smiled.

"Why not? These people gambled their own money so that other people could win."

"One of which wasn't me," Farrell said drily.

McGrew grinned. "You backed the wrong horse."

The Grant girl had been watching them with a faint smile. Now she picked up a newspaper from the top of a barrel. "Are you the Vernon Farrell in this newspaper story?"

"I might be," Farrell said. From ten feet away, he could read the bannerline of the *Oklahoma Warrior*, Dan Hogan's paper:

BEATEN DELEGATE RETURNS FROM WASHINGTON!

Rachel Grant held the paper out to him as he walked over. He took it from her hand and read the story.

> *Vernon Farrell, delegate to Congress for the Five Civilized Tribes and the Cherokee Strip Cattlemen's Association, returns home today, sadder but wiser. We are reliably informed that there will be no "Territory of Cimarron" set aside for cattlemen in the Cherokee Strip.*
>
> *It is the* Warrior's *pleasure to remind its subscribers that the vigilance of its publisher, Dan Hogan, who also spent some time in Washington during this period, was instrumental in preventing a steal of these valuable public lands.*
>
> *We understand a suitable welcome is being planned by Tom Trago and others whose contributions helped finance Farrell's Congressional buggy-ride....*

Farrell laid the paper carefully on a counter, so that he would not crumple and throw it. Old McGrew chuckled. "Let you have both barrels that time, didn't he?"

"No change there," Farrell said drily. Then: "I might as well be getting that gear I left in your shed."

They walked to a shed in the rear. Cole Johnson came along to help carry the hobbles. McGrew had an old saddle which he agreed to lend Johnson for a few days. When they returned to the store, the stagecoach driver had come inside and was having a furtive drink. Farrell made arrangements with him to have his luggage and Johnson's carried to Hogan on the stage.

It was time to get to work. Walking across the dim, cluttered floor, he paid his respects to Rachel Grant.

"Have you got a room arranged for?" he asked her.

"I believe so. I'm sorry about the newspaper story," she said. "It was mean."

"Well, that's Dan Hogan. What drouth and grasshoppers couldn't do in five hundred years, Hogan did in four. He's ruined four-fifths of the Indian Territory. And five days from now they'll fire the cannon that'll ruin the rest of it."

"At least for cattlemen," the girl said.

"For everybody. Ask McGrew."

On the road outside the store, horses could be heard jogging through the soft dust. McGrew looked out. He turned back, looking at Farrell.

"Friends of yours—Tom Trago's bunch. *Now* I bet I'll sell some hard liquor! Lock up your women and valuables, folks!"

The horses stopped before the hitchrack. There was a scuffling of hoofs and a jingling of harness. The homesteaders looked uneasily at each other.

"Who is Tom Trago?" Rachel asked curiously. "He sounds rather fierce."

"He is." Farrell smiled. "Also he's a sort of kinsman of mine. My parents died when I was ten, and an uncle took over. Then the uncle was killed, and his partner inherited me. That was Trago."

Rachel seemed fascinated. "Was your uncle killed by Indians?"

McGrew laughed. He was behind the bar now. "Indians in overalls! He was shot by a homesteader he tried to throw off a claim."

"Tell the rest of it," Farrell said. "The 'claim' was on one of my uncle's grazing leases. But he let him stay there until the man fenced our cattle off from a spring. Then he told him to move along. That was when the squatter shot him."

McGrew grinned as he set out glasses. "And a few days later, Trago shot the homesteader and left him for the coyotes! Tore down his cabin and ran cattle across his fields. A week later, you couldn't 'a' told he'd ever been there."

The homesteaders were listening without a sound. Now there were the voices of the horsemen on the porch.

"You make Trago sound like a Comanche," Vern told McGrew. "But I remember when he used to give the squatters a beef now and then, and let them farm the best bottomlands. But when they started drawing lines we couldn't cross—that's when the love affair ended."

"But that was charity," Rachel said thoughtfully. "I don't defend their fence-building—but what most people want is something of their own. The chance to hold their heads up—not a few acres to farm on sufferance. That's what all these people are here for!"

Farrell said cheerfully, knowing it was over at last and there was no use getting angry about it: "Well, they've got it now. On the sixteenth of September, they'll have all of Oklahoma that's worth having."

Through the door came the somehow ominous sound of boot heels and spur-rowels, and then the slatted door opened quickly and a big man was silhouetted against the blaze of tawny earth. For a moment he was a black pattern—Stetson set on the side of his head, shoulders big and sloping, a gun at his hip. Farrell's eyes adjusted and he took in the hard brown features and the black mustache, like a brigand's—the rough, earthy look of Tom Trago; and he thought, Here is the last of the breed—the cowman who couldn't live with fences. For the kind of country which had produced men like Trago was itself gone now—gelded, branded, and whip-trained.

Trago walked a little way into the room and peered at the group of settlers drinking sarsaparilla. He shuddered.

"Moses and Aaron—they're still comin'!" At last his gaze found Farrell, and a grin cracked the dark face. He slung his old Stetson into the saloon side of the store. "Here's Chief Big Wind himself back from Washington, boys!"

They gripped hands, while the men with Trago came in behind him—Earl Slade, his foreman; Will Motley, another rancher; and Old Man Cuff, who looked like an old Indian in levis, vest, and big black hat. The ranchers gazed at the homesteaders with disdain, and the homesteaders took quick, uneasy glances at them and returned to their quiet conversation.

Farrell scrutinized Trago for the scars left by his months in prison. There were two deep, bitter lines beside his mouth that he did not remember; yet the larger change was something in his bearing, a cold intensification of his natural arrogance, his disdain for anything outside the code he lived by, which was in its essence the survival of the fittest. Trago had had to live for six months in a cage built for men who could not fit themselves into a code designed for tamer men. For six months he had been the caged hawk, forced to eat humility like oatmeal and to bow his head instead of striking out. It would be foolish to think that he had come out the same as he went in. The miracle was that he had been able to deport himself humbly enough to dupe his tormentors into letting him out. But a change had been worked in him, and it was not in the direction of taming him. That much Vern Farrell saw while they gripped hands.

Old Man Cuff walked up and looked at Farrell. His grooved and weathered face was dark as flank-leather. "Fancy town hat—kangaroo boots—how much did all that truck cost us?"

"What did you want me to do?" Farrell asked. "Walk into Congress with manure on my boots and a hat like yours in my hands?"

"Amount you got done," said Earl Slade, Trago's hard-fleshed foreman, "we figured you must have gone in with somebody's hat in your hands."

"I was just four years late," Vern said. "When I got there, it was too late to do anything but buy a ticket home."

He hoped they understood that if they salvaged

anything at all from the wreckage of their empire, it would not be the kind of wind-swept freedom they were accustomed to. Tom Trago looked at him hard, and suddenly Vern was sure that Trago understood nothing except that they had been beaten. Trago turned to the bar and thumped a coin on it.

"Set 'em up, McGrew." He glanced disdainfully at the settlers, and added: "Hell, set 'em up all around! I reckon we can be kind to 'em, can't we—like stray dogs? Have a drink, neighbor?" he asked the young boomer in overalls.

"No, thanks," the man said. Other men shook their heads and one man began examining a cluster of boots hanging from a wall-hook.

Trago's jaw muscles worked. His temper was beginning to work through. "Too strong for your city bellies?" He nudged Old Man Cuff with his elbow. "God, look at 'em, Cuff! Scrawny, crowbait plow-pushers! There ain't a man among 'em!"

"Take it easy," Cuff growled. He was seventy years old, a sturdy little cowman who seldom had much to say, but had a sound and practical mind.

Trago stared at the settlers with rising wrath, and suddenly took a step toward them.

"The Lord damn you back to wherever you came from!" he shouted.

Vern caught his arm as he started across the room. "Come on—we haven't drunk to my homecoming."

Trago yanked free. He gave a cynical smile of tobacco-dyed teeth.

"'Homecoming?' Just what do you call home these days?"

"Oklahoma, till something better shows up."

"Nothing better's going to show up," the rancher, Motley, said pointedly. Motley was a big, heavy-bellied man with a liver-spotted complexion.

"Never can tell," said Vern. But no one seemed to read the implication of his words.

McGrew poured their drinks hastily, smelling trouble

in the wind. Trago picked up his whisky and drank it off neat. He set the glass down and McGrew refilled it. Trago tasted his second drink.

"What *did* you get done back there, aside from chasing floosies and drinking good whisky?" he asked.

Across the room, Vern saw Rachel Grant listening with the fascination of disapproval. "Not much," he admitted.

"Maybe we sent the wrong man," Trago suggested.

"That's possible."

"What about the Territory of Cimarron?" Trago challenged.

"Just a dream—a cowman's heaven where farmers would be off-limits. Well, there is no such place, Tom. There's no miner's territory for miners, no farmer's state for farmers, and there won't be any Territory of Cimarron for cowmen. They laughed me out of the committee room when I suggested it."

"Maybe you laugh out too easy," Trago suggested.

"Listen, Tom," Farrell retorted. "I went back there with my chin out. But I hadn't been there a week when I knew I was just a lamb at a convention of wolves. There was one of me and hundreds of them—about the same proportion as there are cattlemen to homesteaders."

Trago flung his hand in the direction of the boomers, without taking those sour prison-eyes off Vern. "Show me the boomer that's worth a cowman's right hand! Don't talk to me about fight—not in *them* clothes! I showed you how to fight before their damned deputies run me to the ground. If I hadn't had to fight alone, we'd 'a' sent them dragging their tails out of the Territory by now!"

"No, Tom—they'd have had more of us to lock up, that's all."

Trago shut his mouth and looked him over with disdain, thinking of words to express how he felt about men who wouldn't fight. But Old Man Cuff, starting a wheatstraw cigarette, asked pointedly:

"All right—you lost. So where do we go now? If we're done here, where are we going to raise cattle?"

"They said we could apply for government leases in New Mexico or Arizona—almost anywhere but Oklahoma."

"Do we get preference?" Trago demanded.

Farrell shook his head.

"Then what the hell did you get done?" Trago roared. "Nothing! You took a vacation on our money—and came home to crow about it!"

A pulse throbbed in Vern's throat. He faced Trago's anger without trying to parry it. "I'm not crowing. If I failed you, I failed myself. I'm out of business too."

"Are you?" Trago asked drily.

"I haven't any grazing leases left, have I?"

Trago let a small, tight-lipped grin come. "But maybe you picked up a little of the long green in Washington to tide you over."

Vern set down his drink. "I don't get that one."

"Tom's just hoorawin' you," Old Man Cuff muttered. "Come on, Tom—we might as well—"

"I didn't get that one, Tom," Vern repeated.

Trago's dark face sobered. He was not pretending to joke now. "You didn't? I'll make it plain for you. I'm saying you sold us out."

Vern stepped away from the bar. "I owe you quite a bit, but I don't owe you the taking of remarks like that."

"Then don't take it," Trago said.

"Forget it, boys—drink up!" McGrew came in heartily, refilling the glasses. Vern picked up his glass. He looked tight-lipped, competent, and angry.

"I'm telling you to take it back. Don't think I'll swallow that because I'm a shirt-tail nephew of yours."

Trago wiped his mouth, wanting the fight—wanting an adversary he could reach with his fists, not a phantom who lived in Washington, D.C.

"I said you sold us out! You lined your pockets with their money and let them run us out of business! Do you savvy now?"

Vern flicked the glass, and the whisky splashed against

the rancher's face. Trago made a sound like a boar's grunt, a rumble of ferocity and surprise, and he threw his glass aside and came after Vern with his fist cocked, a horn-hard, tough, and desperate man.

CHAPTER 3

Trago hit first and hit hard. His fist collided stunningly with the side of Vern's head. Vern stumbled back, his head ringing. He realized that although he had accepted the challenge, he had not been ready to hit this man who had been like a father to him. He knew that Trago, angry and desperate, needed a small victory to make up for the big fight he had lost.

But Trago was ready. In a country where nearly everything was an enemy, he had existed by always being ready. He kept on top of Vern as he went back, his right fist cocked. Another blow smashed against Vern's ear. Vern tripped and sprawled on his back, aware of the screams of the women.

Trago turned and yanked a coiled whip from a hook on the wall. As Farrell started to his feet, the rancher swung the whip. "Sell us out, eh?" he panted, his dark features veined with rage. He slashed at Vern's head.

Vern threw his hands before his face and the plaited

leather caught his wrist and tore the skin. Trago threw the
whip again and the buckskin popper ripped Vern's shirt.
He stumbled back. The homesteaders were hastily
moving out of the way. A woman cried, "Mr. Johnson—
aren't you going to help him?"

"For five dollars?" Cole Johnson drawled.

Again the rancher swung the whip, but Vern lunged in
unexpectedly and his fist caught Trago high on the
forehead. Trago gave back a step. Farrell hit him solidly
on the mouth. Trago spat blood and a curse, and dropped
the whip. He set himself and loosed a long roundhouse
blow which Farrell ducked. Farrell went inside fast to
grapple with the rancher. Catching him around the neck,
he pivoted and threw Trago on his back. The big, dark
head jarred against the earth floor.

Farrell stepped back, shaken but ready. His fist was
bleeding. He watched Trago roll over, spit blood, and get
to his feet. For a moment the big man hesitated, looking
clearly at him, and Vern peered into his eyes and seemed
to see the old Trago there—the man who had taught him
things about roping, shooting, and survival which no one
else knew. And Trago seemed to look out at him for an
instant, a face across a campfire.

"Come on, Tom—" Vern said softly.

But the face he remembered distorted with a grimace of
anger. The bleeding mouth twisted and Trago came back,
his long left arm stabbing at Vern's face, pushing him
back. Then he swung to Vern's belly, but found the
muscles taut. Farrell dug a short blow to his face and his
nose began to bleed, the blood flowing heavy and dark
over his mouth.

Trago was hurt. A ruby ember of hatred kindled in his
eyes as he pulled his arm back and drove his fist through
Farrell's guard and solidly against his jaw. Farrell went
back against a counter, dazed. The room looked soapy
and out of focus. Trago knew he had hurt him, and he
gathered his strength and drove after him. Vern
side-stepped. The haymaker Trago threw missed and left
him off-balance. For an instant his jaw was exposed.

Farrell struck fast and hard, so hard that his hand ached. He saw the flesh open like beefsteak on Tom Trago's chin.

Trago sank to his knees, his head hanging forward. He looked up, his eyes clearing, and with a sudden gesture he drew his Colt.

Farrell caught his breath and stepped back.

Trago cocked the revolver. A woman screamed and the sound was unnerving. Trago blinked and looked around; then frowned at Farrell and slowly let the gun off-cock. Holstering it, he got up. He pulled out a blue bandanna and put it over his bleeding nose.

Then he looked at his foreman, Slade, and at Old Man Cuff and Will Motley. "Come on, boys," he muttered. "This place stinks of Congressmen and boomers."

As they started out, Farrell said: "Don't you want to know how I spent your money in Washington?"

"Be a great comfort," said Earl Slade. "Later."

"Come around if you want to know. I'll be camped south of town tonight with a herd of horses."

The men went out. The homesteaders stared at Farrell, who caught the bar-towel McGrew tossed him and began wiping the blood from his face. He felt sick, drained, emotionally depleted. He was disgusted, having knocked himself out for four months for his friends, only to come back to a welcome like this. He saw Cole Johnson standing beside the borrowed saddle, and fished a goldpiece from his pocket and flipped it to him.

"You're paid off," he said.

Johnson buffed the brim of his hat with his sleeve. "What's the matter—did you want me to mix in it too? It looked like a family affair, and I never mix in family fights."

Farrell grunted. "I thought maybe you'd had enough of ranch-life. Come along, if you've a mind."

He found his hat among the sacks on the floor, nodded to Rachel Grant, settled with McGrew, and went out the door. Soon after, he heard Johnson following him.

CHAPTER 4

An hour later, lurching along in the stagecoach, Rachel Grant was still sick with reaction from the fight. She thought of how the two men had looked, their faces and clothing blood-smeared, as they smashed at each other with their fists. And she was queasy too when she thought of the next few hours before her, and of all the things which might happen.

The stagecoach had been moving slowly for a time, while the driver let the horse rest. The heat of the rolling prairie with its small, burned-out farms was suffocating. But now she felt the wheels rolling faster, and a moment later the driver leaned down to shout:

"Hogan—end of the line, folks!"

End of the line. She smiled to herself. Indeed it was! End of the line—for Daniel Hogan!

The stage swept down the side of a vast and unbelievably cluttered town square. She stared at the great, gray, gypsy-like camp. Four streets of ramshackle

27

buildings bounded a square several acres in extent, every square yard occupied by a wagon, a tent, or a clothesline. It was a dusty canvas jungle where men and women could be seen carrying buckets of water, handing up wash on lines strung between wagons, tending horses, or minding children. The stage turned a corner, ran along another side of the square, and came rocking to a halt before the stage depot. The numbing reaction of the past three days of travel nearly overpowered the girl. She closed her eyes and waited until someone said, "All out, miss!"

Rachel got out. A tall man in his shirtsleeves was trying to sell maps to the other passengers. "—All the mile corners and surveyors' monuments plainly marked, folks! Includes the location of the townsite of Pawnee, the next boomtown in the Cherokee Strip! Plus full information as to the taking of claims."

Several of the passengers bought maps. Rachel checked her bags with the baggage-master. "Can you tell me where to find the newspaper office?" she asked him.

"We've got three papers, miss. Which one?"

"The *Warrior*."

"The big one." The baggage-master smiled. "Walk east to the corner and turn left. It's halfway up the east side of the square."

In the yellow heat she walked to the corner. She could not take her eyes from that huge encampment in the square. It exuded misery, somehow, as it gave off dust. A single large elm tree stood among the wagons. Otherwise there was no shade anywhere, not a blade of green. Nothing but dust, smoke, flies, and heat. Children could be heard crying. Horses stamped and switched at flies. The women all seemed to be busy, bent over a washboard or a kettle, but most of the men appeared to be sitting about, waiting. Their work would come later.

Where in the world, she wondered, could all these people be put? Everyone could not possibly win a claim. Would they divide up the claims again to take care of the ones who lost out? If they didn't, where would they go? How would they get home again, if they had spent everything to come to Oklahoma to gamble for land?

Perhaps that man Trago was right. Perhaps it was wrong to try to move a population onto an Indian reservation in one mighty, heartbreaking rush.

She found the *Warrior* office in almost the only brick building on the square. The whole town had a look of impermanence. She counted—this was a special interest of hers—eleven saloons between the stage depot and the office of the *Warrior*. There were cement curbs, but the dirt walks were worn deep. Here and there a striped awning formed a brief oasis of shade. She passed the town fire department, a tall building with a fire-bell in a cradle on the sidewalk before it.

Reaching the office of the *Oklahoma Warrior*, Rachel entered it and inspected the interior closely. It looked shabbily prosperous, with a cluttered counter separating the customers' side and some oaken banks of type-cases. There were maps on the walls, and boomers' slogans everywhere. A sample of every handbill printed in four years had been pasted up. Bundles of newspapers bound with binder-twine were stacked on the floor. Cigar smoke rocked in layers on the still air, and there was a hot reek like that of a laundry—the breath of a steam-boiler somewhere. From the rear came the hiss and clank of a press.

The rear work-area was separated from the front by a partition which rose short of the ceiling. An opening in it was draped with an old monk's-cloth curtain. From behind this curtain came a man's voice, deep and rough:

"I wouldn't give a dime for a square *block* of this town next week. Not a dime! Everything's going to be Pawnee! A river and a railroad. Pawnee, Oklahoma! For once the government put the townsite where the big town's going to be."

She felt a ripple of excitement at the voice. She had not thought she would remember it.

Another man said, "Fine way to talk about the town that was named after you, Dan."

"It should be named Cirrhosis, the number of saloons it's got."

"It'll be different this time. We'll license the saloons

and limit the number of them. Organization! That's the whole key."

Rachel conjectured. Hogan must be holding a strategy meeting with some of the select group which the old man at Osage had spoken of. She saw a push-bell on the counter and tapped it.

The curtain moved aside. She had a glimpse of a room where four men sat about a table in shirt-sleeves. Maps and papers littered it. She could see the broad back of a big man with thick white hair and a brown neck. He was waving a hand that held a cigar. Even after fifteen years, Rachel recognize that gesture.

A long, thin man with a sallow face and sad, bespectacled eyes came through the opening, wiping his hands on a piece of waste. Rachel smelled benzine and whisky on him.

"I'd like to place an announcement in the paper," she said.

From beneath the counter, the printer took a yellow block of paper. "To run how many times?"

"Indefinitely. I have the copy right here—"

From the tapestry bag she carried, she extracted a leaflet. It was headed:

WOULD YOU SELL YOUR SOUL
FOR A DRINK OF WHISKY?

The printer rubbed his chin. He measured the column of type with a steel ruler. Tilting his head, he warned:

"Gonna cost a lot, ma'am.—How many times did you say?"

"Indefinitely."

Behind the partition, Dan Hogan was declaiming: "But the speculators don't know the surveyors' corners! Racehorses be damned. I'll *walk* our people to the good claims before those boys on their fancy sprinters find the first half-dozen monuments!"

"—It'd have to be paid for in advance for one week, ma'am," the printer warned.

Rachel touched her cheek in perplexity. "Oh—oh, that's too bad! Is that the publisher of the paper in back there? Mr. Hogan, I think his name is?"

"Yes, ma'am, but he's—"

"Please tell him a lady from Harmony, Indiana, would like to speak to him."

Regarding the temperance leaflet skeptically, the printer shrugged: "It ain't the kind of copy he's like to run free of charge, miss."

"You mean Mr. Hogan—drinks?"

"Never takes a drop. But he ain't opposed to other folks having a nip."

"So I gathered." Rachel smiled, with an audible sniff. "Please tell him I'd like a word, however."

The printer went behind the curtain, and the conversation ended. There was a shocked silence. Then a man said: "What's the matter, Dan? You all right?" A chair scraped, and Rachel felt her heart ballooning with excitement. She was sure it was he; and yet she had to be absolutely certain before she went any further.

A very large man came into the curtained doorway. His thick white hair somehow enhanced the vigor of a brown face cut with deep lines. His eyes were blue and keen, and they searched Rachel's face before he moved toward the counter. The printer started to follow him, but Hogan waved the cigar flaccidly.

"I'll take care of the lady, Fred."

Dan Hogan smiled, with tears in his eyes, and reached for the girl's hand. She pulled it away.

"Rachel!" he said. "I thought sure it would be your mother."

She found she could not meet his eyes. She bit her lip and frowned at the temperance tract.

"I'm interested in having this printed in your paper."

"Rachel," he said, reprovingly. "Don't you know me?"

Her lips were trying to tremble. She firmed them and steadfastly gazed into his face. "If you don't want the business," she said, "I'll have to take it elsewhere. But I'll leave a few leaflets with you, if you don't mind."

Dan Hogan chuckled. "My daughter a reformer? Oh, no! Rachel, tell me about your mother. How is she?"

Her mother was dead only a month, but Rachel was not going to tell him that until the proper time. "Good day," she said, taking a step away from the counter.

Hogan lifted the counter-gate and came after her. His large hand closed on her wrist.

"Now, see here! Don't be silly. I know you, young woman, even if you were only six when I saw you last. You've got your mother's hair and eyes, but my chin—and don't be trying to use that chin on me. Now, where are you staying?"

"How could I be your daughter, Mr. Hogan? My name is Grant."

Hogan dropped his voice. "All right, so is mine, so is mine! I suppose you saw my picture somewhere?"

She did not reply. Her chin up, she turned and gazed out the door.

"—I don't suppose you'd be interested in why I left?" Hogan murmured.

"Left? Which time?" she said bitterly. "I'm primarily interested in why you didn't come back."

"I couldn't, that's all! I had to make a clean break. It wasn't something I wanted to do—I *had* to do it!"

"Had to? No one *has* to do anything that will hurt another person."

"My dear young woman!" Hogan said drily. "Whether or not it hurts someone else is beside the point, when you *have* to do something. I had to get out from under that house full of children and domesticity! It was choking me—"

"When you were only home every six months? It seems to me you had quite a full life—fighting Indian wars, goldmining, scouting—"

"And bleeding inside, so that I had to come home every few months to be with you all! But damn it—some men aren't made to live like housebroken animals! I could have settled down and gone to fat—or I could leave and do the things I had to. I sent money whenever I could. I

still send it, you know that. It's not much, I admit, and of
course for quite a while I couldn't send anything. I was—"
He picked up one of the leaflets. "I was selling my soul for
a drink of whisky. Every fifteen minutes. For five years,"
he added.

"Why?" she asked.

"Because I'm weak. Oh, you couldn't tell that to those
boomers behind the curtain there. I'm only weak in the
important things, you see. Like steadiness and responsibility—things like that.—How is your mother, Rachel?"

"You'll hear about it all—at the appropriate time."

Pulling her arm from his grip, she started out. Dan
Hogan kept step with her and held both arms from
behind. "Rachel—is this all you wanted to say? About my
deserting?" It was in his voice—the real fear she knew he
had been hiding. How much of his final leave-taking did
she know?

"Let me go," she said.

"Not until—"

"I'm going to scream for help," Rachel said. "And that
won't do the Great White Father of all those boomers
much good, will it? They'll have to look for another
father—as we did."

Hogan's hands dropped away. She walked from the
shop.

On the assumption that the office of the town marshal
would be somewhere on the square, she walked to the
corner and found it next to a large saloon, the Cherokee
Bar. She went into the small office. Three men were
playing cards around a table consisting of a board placed
on the top of a small heat-stove. One of them, she
supposed, must be the marshal, though there was no
badge in view. A rough-looking man in shirt-sleeves and
suspenders laid down his cards and stood up. His
unshaven jowls looked as greasy and dark as the
back-side of a flitch of bacon.

"Yes, ma'am," he said. "What can we do for you?"

"Are you the town marshal?"

"Marshal Welty, at your service."

The other card-players grinned. Welty had no look of daring about him, no cold blue eye. He was big and ox-like.

"I'm Rachel Grant. I'd like to have a man arrested."

The other card-players stood up, as if she had now established her rights as a lady. Marshal Welty directed a frown of embarrassment at the other men. "Why don't you boys take a walk around the block?"

Rachel shook her head. "It's not that kind of case. No one has molested me." From her bag she took a folded paper and an envelope. "I have here a warrant for the arrest of one Daniel Grant, *alias* Daniel Hogan, a former resident of Harmony, Indiana."

The men looked perfectly blank; then shocked; then they began to smile. Rachel opened the envelope.

"And I have here documents and photographs attesting the fact that Daniel Hogan is Daniel Grant; that he was married to my mother, Susan Grant, now deceased; and that he is sought on a number of counts of failure to provide, as well as evading arrest."

Half amused, half irritated, the marshal looked the warrant over. He scratched his ear.

"Do you know who Daniel Hogan is?" he asked.

Rachel nodded. "I've just been speaking with him. I wanted to be sure I had the right man."

"Well, I ain't so sure I can even *arrest* a man on charges like that. . . ."

"I also have a warrant charging second-degree murder," Rachel said, "which I think will empower you to make an arrest."

The men looked at each other. There was a vibration in the room—an air of being present at a scene which would make history, local if not national. Marshal Welty tucked in his shirt-tail.

"Now, let's just back up a mite—" he began.

"Marshal, are you *afraid* to arrest Daniel Hogan?"

"No. But I'd think twice about bringing charges, if I was you."

"Is he so dangerous as all that?" The girl smiled.

"No, but some of his people might get violent. They're counting on him to lead them to the good claims on Opening Day. Some of the men who've supported him—important men, you see."

"Nothing is more important than justice," Rachel said.

Welty scratched his scalp, picked up his cards for some reason and consulted them, and at last decided: "Well, it won't hurt to *ask* Dan if he's the same feller."

Rachel smiled and dropped the legal-looking papers back in her bag.

CHAPTER 5

Two miles south of Hogan lay an area which had proved too rough even for a homesteader's plow. A stream which lived a brief but violent life every spring had ripped deep gullies through the rolling plain. Giant old pecan trees and elms grew along the brushy bottomlands; withered blackberry thickets sheltered a multitude of birds and small game. The soil would grow anything, but heavier equipment than a homesteader's was needed to fill the gullies, grub out the deep-rooted trees, and level the land.

To a cattleman like Farrell, it seemed like heaven.

They put the horses on the short-grass late that afternoon, leaving them chain-hobbled. The hobbles were short lengths of chain fixed to a foreleg by a leather strap. The horse could walk without panicking at finding its legs tethered, but if it tried to run, a slap or two of the chain against its free leg was enough to bring it back to a walk. Under the trees there were pools and a little running water.

Farrell had cleaned up. He was bruised from his battle with Tom Trago, and the side of his face felt feverish and swollen. He was despondent at how things had gone at Osage. Trago had been like a father to him—a rough and cavalier father, true—but it was hard to accept that they should be enemies now. But Trago was desperate, having lost not merely a trade, but a world, and the logical man to vent his desperation on was Vern.

When Vern had left Osage with the horses, he had made up his mind that they would have to come to him if they wanted to hear about his plan for survival. But his resolution began to weaken. Trago had acted in anger, and by now he would be trying to decide how to apologize without using the humble words. He would be in the Cherokee Bar, no doubt, telling Old Man Cuff:

"He should 'a' known I didn't mean it that way," and, "I only drew the gun because I thought he was drawing his..."

He touched his swollen lip and grinned to himself, remembering Trago bluffing out the cavalry when they tried to put him off Indian land he had forgotten to lease; Trago walking into a saloon full of men who had sworn to get back at him for something, and walking out untouched; Trago putting sticks under his blankets at night during Indian trouble, so that he would not sleep too heavily...

Oh, hell, he decided, it won't cost anything to give him a chance to make his manners.

As he was preparing to ride to town, Cole Johnson and Bill Spence rode in from the horse-herd, looking hot and flushed. Farrell had hung a little steel mirror from a projection of a tree-trunk. He was shaving before it as they pulled up.

"Okay, that's five dollars' worth," said Johnson, leaning on the saddle-swell.

"How'd you like to make another two hundred dollars?"

Johnson looked at the swellings on Vern's face. "Not if I've got to fight Trago's bunch to earn it."

"No fights. Trago's all right—we just got off on the wrong foot. I like your company, boys—about two hundred dollars' worth."

"What makes horse-herdin' so tough in Oklahoma?" Spence asked.

"Let's say I'm offering ten dollars for the first three days, and a hundred and ninety for the fourth."

"You wouldn't be wanting somebody to ride your mounts in the Opening, would you, now?" smiled Johnson. "That wouldn't be legal, Mister Farrell."

"Don't tell me, then, and spoil all my fun. I just came from Washington, where they wrote the rules, and I say it would. All I want is some men to ride a horse and pound a stake on the Sixteenth."

Johnson shrugged. "I'm agreeable."

"Okay," Spence said.

"I'll ride into town, then, and bring out some supplies. I'll fetch your warsacks from the stage depot. I've got a wagon and a camp outfit at a stable."

He rode the two miles to Hogan in the smoky twilight. Here and there in a field could be seen a settler's outfit, a wagon and tent and a horse or two. As he neared the town he saw more of these impoverished-looking morsels of civilization, and a number of men hiking along the road. Some of them carried water-buckets which they had filled in town.

Farrell rode up Kickapoo Street to the square and halted, staring in disbelief at the transformation of the sinful but quiet little town of Hogan. The sun was going down, suffocating in red dust. Canvas tents and shelters nearly covered the five-acre town square. Canvas taut, and canvas loose—all of it fluttering in the evening wind, shaking out the dust of the day. Wood-smoke mingled with the dust. Men, women, and children carried buckets of water back and forth from the horse-troughs and pumps adjacent to the square. There must have been five thousand settlers camped in that square, he thought. Five thousand miserable beings, come to make the land itself miserable.

He saw a tree he remembered—the only tree in the square, now.

On that very spot he had shot a prairie wolf five years before, when he was a salty youngster of nineteen working with Tom Trago. The wolf had been dragging down Trago's calves, and Vern had finally managed to kill it and bring it into camp, a little proud of himself. Trago had winked at the punchers around the fire and said:

"Ain't it a tough little rooster? Kills it a stray settler's dog and crows fit to be heard clean across the Injun Territory!"

Vern shook the wolf out of his loop, stared at Trago in black anger, and rode away.

And now he looked out on this piece of ground which had once been cattle-range, and remembered those times with affection—the times of free range, blanket Indians, and a no-quarter cattle trade. For that kind of ranching was gone. A smart man would work out a plan and try to make it work.

Farrell's plan pivoted on townsites.

The town of Pawnee—so designated on the government maps—was certain to be the next boom-town of the whole Territory. It was watered by Pawnee Creek, an all-year stream, and a railroad was going to pass through it. All about this mythical town of Pawnee were level plains of rich wheat land. This was going to be the town, and Farrell and some other men with fast horses, plus previous knowledge of where the old stone monuments lay in the grass, were going to take those townsites for their own. To build stores on, borrow on, or speculate with.

Most of the stores in Hogan were just closing. He bought provisions, picked up the wagon he had left at a stable months ago, collected the provisions, and secured the luggage he had sent in on the stage. It was dark now. He had an idea he might find some of his old riders at the Cherokee Bar. Most of them would be needing work, and the proposition he had to offer them would be like found money. He left the wagon at the stable and walked to the saloon.

Next door to the Cherokee, Marshal Welty was leaning against the brick wall of the jail, smoking a cigar in the hot summer evening. Welty was a homesteader's man, and he gave Farrell a long, expressionless stare as he passed.

Farrell went into the saloon. He took a breath of the dust and smoke, and smiled. It was almost like the old days in a cowtown saloon. Half the men in the place wore Stetsons and spurs. In one glance he saw a dozen punchers he knew. And he saw them recognize him, and begin working out their little speeches asking about prospects. . . .

As he walked along the bar, a man spoke to him from a table. "That was some good-lookin' horseflesh you brought in."

He stopped and looked at the man. It was Earl Slade, Tom Trago's hatchet-faced foreman. Slade was drinking with Old Man Cuff and Will Motley. Trago was not with them. They had a bottle of whisky on the table and some papers on which they had been figuring.

"They'll do," Farrell agreed.

Motley, a big, soft-spoken man, had a stub of pencil in his fingers, and there was a piece of paper before him with columns of figures and calculations all terminating in the proposition that a cowman could no longer make a living in Oklahoma. Motley paused to push his spectacles up on his forehead.

"Cow-horses?" he asked.

"No. Just usin'-horses," Vern said.

Old Man Cuff gave his faint, sourish smile. He looked like a town-Indian in his high black Stetson. "Sit down, boy. Have a drink."

"Maybe one," Vern said.

He laid his hat on the table. Motley turned the papers over as if they contained a secret which Farrell must not be let in on until his intentions were known. Earl Slade got up. "I'll get a glass," he said.

In a moment he was back with a wet whisky glass. They

poured, raised glasses and touched them.

"To corn-weevils and crop failures," Old Man Cuff toasted.

"I'll drink to that."

They drank. Then there was an awkward silence. "...Usin'-horses," said Motley thoughtfully. "Say—old Duncan's around town. He could train 'em up for you about as quick as anybody."

Vern smiled. "I expect. Where's Trago?"

"Out rangin' the town, I reckon, looking for a boomer that thinks he's tough."

"Trago'd better get civilized. They civilized the Indian, they civilize horses, and somebody's going to civilize him one of these days. I thought maybe prison would have tamed him down a little."

Old Man Cuff swirled his drink thoughtfully. "Tom's a mite hard to understand lately," he agreed. "Maybe prison changed him—it shore didn't tame him."

"How did he make out?"

"He's never said a word, and we knowed him better than to ask. But hell! How's a wolf make out in a cage? He breaks his teeth on the bars and wears his paws down to the flesh trying to dig through the concrete. But if he ever gets out—man, nobody's ever going to take him back again."

"Nobody's trying to," Vern said.

"Same thing, to his way of figuring—locking him up, or putting him out of business." Cuff's wise, sad gaze came up. "I've got a little of that wolf-blood myself. I know what he's feeling. He's still buckin' the idea that we're through here. We all figured you'd have something to suggest when you came back. Tom was kind of took aback when you didn't."

"I do have. Nobody gave me a chance to tell about it."

Old Man Cuff squinted at him. They were silent a moment, waiting for someone to ask it. "What would that be, now?" Cuff asked.

"It might be a good idea if Trago asked me," Vern said.

The saloon doors opened and a young fellow in town clothes, big and sturdy and with dark hair curling from under his pushed-back hat, walked inside and looked the place over. He resembled a man who had had several drinks and had come to announce that he could whip any man in the place. His features were ruddy and strong, with a reckless strain in them.

"Jeff Ridge—Hogan's errand boy," Motley chuckled. "God, ain't he wild!"

"What's the matter with him?" Vern asked. "They're winning all the hands, aren't they?"

"Didn't you hear about Hogan?" Slade asked, incredulously.

Vern looked at him blankly. But Ridge was coming down the room, staring straight at Farrell. He knew him as a sort of orderly and color sergeant in Daniel Hogan's army. He stopped near the table and glared at him. There was angry blood in his face.

"Anybody found the Great White Father yet?" Motley asked Slade, ignoring Ridge.

"By God, we'll see you in jail for this!" Ridge shouted. He was staring furiously at Vern.

Vern looked around to be sure Ridge was talking to him. "For what? Do I need a note from my mother to drink in this town?"

"You know what I'm talking about! You dug up that chippy and sicced her on him!"

Vern looked at the others. "Anybody know what he's talking about?"

"I'll show you what I'm talking about!" Ridge said, and he swung hard at Farrell's head.

The blow hit him high on the forehead and knocked him over in the chair. Before he could rise, Slade and several cowboys had nailed Ridge against the bar. Slade's fist jarred against his jaw and Jeff Ridge began to slide down. Then another puncher hit him and he fell to his hands and knees. Vern got up and pulled Slade back.

"What's the matter with him? Is he crazy? What's the damn fool talking about?"

On the floor, Ridge occupied a little space by himself. He got up dazedly. Men were maneuvering to watch the fight if one developed. Vern saw some settlers working in

close to stand behind Ridge, as Slade and several of the
cow-crowd began to bunch together.

"What's the matter?" Farrell asked the man.

Ridge's face worked. "You don't know nothing about
it, eh? You came in on the same train with her—but you
don't know why she came to Hogan!"

Vern looked at Slade. The foreman pushed his hat over
one ear and grinned at Jeff Ridge. "I reckon you were out
of town when it happened," he told Vern. "Some woman
swore out a warrant for Hogan for second-degree murder
this afternoon."

Vern blinked. "Was her name Rachel Grant?"

"That was it, I think. Hogan took off before Welty
could arrest him. This is going to make a little change in
Hogan's plan for the Opening, eh?"

"You just think it is!" said the young boomer
breathlessly. "We'll have that girl in jail, and him free,
before the Opening!"

A sort of gambler, she had told Vern she was. She had
seemed to know where she was going, too. Didn't need a
room. Everything was arranged.

"... Second-degree murder," he said to the homesteader. "I'd call it first-degree, what he's done to
Oklahoma."

Another man came in the door, a tall and grave-
looking man named Myron Tackett, Hogan's lawyer. He
looked the scene over, and Vern sensed that he had been
summoned quickly from Hogan's headquarters. He
spoke in a sharp, commanding voice.

"Come on, Jeff. Let's go."

Ridge looked around, glowered at Vern and the others,
and hitched up his pants. "We ain't through," he said.
"We ain't even started!"

"Maybe you ain't even going to start," Slade jeered.

Ridge went out with the lawyer.

Vern found himself thinking about the girl. He picked
up his hat from the table. "I'm camped down on
Comanche Creek, if Trago wants to talk to me. I'll see
you, boys."

CHAPTER 6

By night the tent-city looked quite colorful, with fires blazing in the dark and lamps glowing softly under canvas. Farrell saw a man with a doctor's bag accompanying a settler into the tents. Somebody sick. How an epidemic would travel in that jungle! How a fire would leap from tent to tent. And what was ahead of most of these people, anyway, but more misery?

Someone was working in the *Warrior* office. The roller-shades were drawn halfway to the top, but he could see where a lamp resting on a desk threw a glow against the ceiling. He knocked. There was a pause; then a voice:

"Who is it?"

"Vernon Farrell."

The door was unlatched and he glanced into the shop. In the lamplight, the girl's hair gleamed reddish-gold. She wore a white shirtwaist with a little gold watch pinned to it, and a dark, tube-like skirt. Paper cuffs were pinned to her sleeves. She looked slender and most attractive; for a reformer, unbelievably so.

"Will you come in?" she said. The invitation seemed a step removed from enthusiasm.

Farrell walked in. "I had to come to town, and I thought I'd see if you'd found a room."

"How did you find me?"

"A man up the street told me where to find you."

She smiled. "Fred, the printer?"

"No—Jeff Ridge, the boomer. They're mighty hot about this, Miss Rachel."

"I'm sorry, but—'sticks and stones—'" she quoted.

"Sticks and stones are what I'm thinking about." Vern touched his forehead, where Ridge had struck him.

"For heaven's sake!" she exclaimed, gazing at the bruise.

"For *your* sake, Miss Rachel. Ridge thinks I brought you here to use against Hogan. Does that qualify me to ask what you're up to?"

Drifting to the desk, Rachel adjusted the wick of the lamp. She seemed to weigh the matter. Then, turning the chatelaine watch, she glanced at the time.

"It's late, and I have an editorial to finish. But I'll tell you briefly how I happen to be running the *Warrior*. Daniel Hogan's real name is Grant. He's my father. I saw his picture in a newspaper a few weeks ago, and a few inquiries convinced me it was the same man who deserted my mother fifteen years ago."

"Do they jail a man for desertion?"

"The jailing was for second-degree murder. On his last visit home, he killed a man who was boarding with us."

Vern frowned. "Hogan did that? He must have been drunk."

"Appetites have always dominated Daniel Hogan. When he *did* come home, he'd always start drinking in a short time. Then he'd begin abusing my mother, and finally he'd disappear again. He'd send us a little money from time to time, but by and large, it was my mother's needle which supported us."

"And now," Vern said, "you've got him."

"Got him? I don't look at it that way. I do think people

should have to stand trial for murder, don't you?"

"Sure, but—Well, if I'd been away, and came back to find a man in my bedroom, I'd probably lose my temper too."

"The man wasn't in his bedroom. He was in the spare bedroom."

Farrell considered. She had a point. Yet murder seemed out of character for old Dan Hogan, whose best friends and worst enemies were ideas. But there was a zealot's light in the girl's eyes, and he decided to stay out of an argument with her.

"So now you've disposed of the old rascal." He smiled. "What happens next?"

"I'll run the paper for a while. I expect the court will award it to me."

On the counter were neat little stacks of leaflets. He looked at one of them. *"Would you sell your soul for a drink of whisky?"* he read and chuckled. "So the old *Warrior*'s going to be turned into a reform sheet!"

"Perhaps you can suggest a worthier use for it?"

Farrell gazed at her thoughtfully, and shook his head. "You'll never stick it out. Not a good-looking woman like you."

Rachel glanced at her watch in annoyance, her face turning faintly pink. "And what has my physical appearance to do with it?"

"I've got a theory about reformers. I never saw a lady reformer yet who wasn't as homely as a mud hen-house. So the homely girls kind of lump men and whisky as evils, and begin campaigning in all directions. But just let a man propose to one of them, and a lot of temperance tracts are going to start mildewing in the basement."

Rachel's eyes flashed. "The old, old story! If a woman wants to improve the world, it must be because she can't get a man. *Oh—!*"

There was a splintering crash from one of the windows. Rachel screamed and clutched at him. Something struck the desk-lamp, which burst apart in a glistening lake of coal oil and shards of glass. Blue-and-yellow flames flickered up and down the side of it, feeding on the spilled oil on the floor. Rachel screamed again and backed away from the flames, pulling her skirts to her knees.

Vern looked for a water-bucket. There was none, but he saw a printer's apron hanging from a hook. He yanked it loose and threw it over the desk, snuffing out the fire on the desk-top. From the floor, however, flames licked up the side of the desk, while a greasy smoke of burning wood began to stain the clean coal-oil flame. He started to pull off his jacket to throw it over the fire. The shop was lighted by the uneven, gurgling pulsations of the flames. Then he saw the monk's-cloth curtain between the front and rear sections of the shop, and he ducked under the counter to tear it down. He threw it over the flames on the floor and with his hat beat out the fire beginning to erode the side of the desk. The flames were out. A smoky darkness filled the shop.

Men were running up the street. A moment later someone pounded on the door. "Anyone in there?" a man shouted.

"Open the back windows!" Vern told Rachel. "Let's get some air in here." He unlatched the door.

"It's all right now," he told the breathless man who stood on the walk. Several others joined him. Along the near edge of the boomer camp, men and boys had gathered to stare at the building. One of them, probably, had thrown the rock which had started the fire, one of Hogan's partisans, resentful over the accusation against the messiah of the landless.

The men on the walk were trying to see inside the print-shop. "What happened?" one of them asked.

"Just an accident. A lamp was broken. We can handle it now."

He closed the door. Stepping to the window, he drew the roller-shades all the way up, then struck a match and began looking for a lamp. Rachel returned from opening the back door. In the dim match-light, she moved to a wall-light and struck a match. She raised the chimney of the lamp and held it to the wick. He watched her, fascinated. She looked beautiful, with the yellow light dusting her hair and her profile clean as the cameo of a silver coin. When the lamp was lighted, she lowered the chimney and turned to look at him. Placing one hand on her breast, she took a deep breath, and smiled:

"Heavens!"

"The reformer's lot is a hard one," Farrell said.

"This had nothing to do with reformation. This was revenge, plain and simple."

"However you figure it, you'd better close up shop until after the Opening."

Rachel tilted her chin. "I'll do no such thing. In the next few days I can reach a lot of people in this town. From all I hear, there won't be any town of Hogan left after the Opening. If I can just send those people out with some worthwhile thoughts—something to hold to after they establish their new homes! . . ."

She gazed toward the square, her face aglow. She seemed to muse on all those damaged souls out there, contemplating them like a cabinet-maker given carte-blanche to restore a whole wrecking-yard full of ruined furniture to new condition.

"What is it you don't like—men or whisky?" Farrell asked.

Rachel smiled reproachfully. "I'm not nearly so narrow as you think," she said. "But we've had hard times in my family, and most of it seems to stem directly from my father's drinking. So it seems natural to be striking a blow at intemperance. Is that so hard to understand?"

"No. I don't blame you. I just don't think you can shotgun people into reforming. I think you have to coax them, and you can't coax a hundred at a time. Look at Bill Spence, this little cowpoke I hired at K.C. He'd been drunk six weeks when I found him. Do you think reading a tract would keep him from going on another bender when the spell was on him?"

"I don't know," Rachel said thoughtfully. "But if I have the opportunity, I'm just liable to put one in his hands.—You've been very kind, Mr. Farrell," she said, smiling, but suddenly brisk. "Do look in on me when you're in town, won't you?"

Clearly, the meeting was over. He tasted a sharp disappointment. He put his hand out and she gave him hers.

"I will. I sure will," he said. "In the meantime, keep those shades drawn."

At the livery stable, he tied his saddle-horse to the wagon while the hostler hitched his team. He tucked the tarpaulin securely over the load on the flat-bed. He had already paid his board-bill on the horses, and he drove down the alley and turned south into the country. In the thickets beside the road, crickets made a singing clamor. Out in the dark, dry, sun-stricken fields homesteaders had their little camps where the bunch-grass had grown four years ago. Four years! And in those years things had happened to the country which could never be undone.

He heard a sound behind him—a rustling under the tarpaulin. He turned his head, thinking that one of the stable cats had fallen asleep in the wagon. The canvas was suddenly thrown back and a man reared to his knees. Farrell was shocked. In the dim star-shine he recognized the rutted, dark face and white hair of Dan Hogan.

"Just keep drivin', Congressman," Hogan said. "You and me are going to have a talk."

CHAPTER 7

There was something remote in Daniel Hogan, something lost, and at times his expression was like that of a man thinking about getting drunk. He was always busy, eternally going somewhere or coming from somewhere, and it had often seemed to Farrell that he kept on the go in order not to have time to think too much.

His face was full of this discontent as he crouched on the wagon behind Vern, touching a spot between his shoulders with something which might have been a stick, but was probably a gun. Vern could not be sure.

"How did you know I was leaving town?" he asked.

"Ridge told me. For what you've done to me," Hogan growled, "I should blow your brains from here to Kansas."

"I never saw the girl before she got on the train."

"Oh, hell—I'm too old for nursery tales! Did you pay her to come out? Or is she in it for what the shop's worth?"

"Ask Rachel. She seems to be in it for a printing press and a couple of thousand lost souls."

"How did you find her? Did you hire the Pinkertons to investigate me?"

"You're not too old for nursery tales," Vern said wryly. "You're telling yourself one right now."

"All right," Hogan grumbled, "she's here. What will you take to call her off?"

"All I know about that girl is she's death on sin. And it seems to me like you're a sinner from 'way back."

"I'm all of that. But I'm not a murderer."

"Maybe I listen to the wrong rumors," Farrell said.

Hogan moved around and the pressure on Vern's back eased a little. But when he tried to draw away from it, Hogan said sharply:

"Set still and keep drivin'! I'm going to tell you about it, just to set the record straight. I'd been away from home for over a year. My business kept me traveling those days. I came home late at night that time and walked into one of my boys' bedrooms, figuring to catch some sleep on the floor and not bother my wife until morning. I was looking for a blanket in the dark when somebody piled out of bed and began yelling at me. I told him who I was, but the damned fool started firing at me! I didn't know who he was. But I had to defend myself. I hit him. He went down and the gun went off. Evidently the bullet hit him. I took off. I knew I'd be in trouble if they found me there."

"You were in trouble anyway. Why didn't you stick around and explain yourself?"

Hogan sighed. "All right—I was drunk! I lost my head. Of course like a damned, drunken fool I left my suitcase behind. So I had to buy the longest ticket I could afford and change my name."

"If that's the case, what are you worrying about? Go back to Indiana and explain it to them. If it was his gun, you're clear."

"Fine!" said Hogan, bitterly. "But that doesn't help my bunch in Oklahoma, does it? When that cannon goes off, I've got to lead them to Pawnee!"

"What's so special about them? You can't lead everybody to Pawnee."

"I'm not trying to lead everybody—just a little gang of about fifty men I owe what you might call an election debt to. It cost a lot of money to push this thing through Congress. There was plenty of big money offered me, but I went after the little money—the good farmers without much capital, the merchants and bankers with a few hundred dollars to invest. The ones who could make Oklahoma solid and respectable. They sank their money in a double gamble: a chance that we'd get the Cherokee Strip—and a long chance that they'd get claims when it was opened. I couldn't promise them anything. Some of them hardly have two dimes to rub together now."

"That's more than they'll have after the first winter."

"The Lord and the weather will have something to say about that, Farrell," Hogan snapped.

"The Lord said, No, last time," Vern reminded him. "Because we've had the rottenest weather in forty years. And we haven't found the right crop yet."

Vern pulled the horses in. When the soft shuffle of their hoofs died, he could hear horses jogging far behind them. Hogan's head turned. He spoke angrily, "Get this thing moving!" As the wagon lurched forward again, Hogan began talking more urgently.

"I haven't got all night. I want to make a deal with you. I hear you brought in a herd of horses. What for?"

"That's *my* little secret."

"Secret, hell! I can see through you on a cloudy day! You think you're going to hire men to take claims for you. Well, my friend, it's not legal. The homestead laws give one claim to a customer—and he has to live on it for five years before it's his to dispose of."

"Unless he commutes," Vern said.

"Commutes?" Hogan echoed. It had the hollow sound of a stone dropped in a well. He knew the word all too well.

The horses were not far behind. The time seemed right to let Hogan catch the fish he was desperately trying to hook.

"I didn't waste *all* my time in Washington," Vern said.

"A couple of lawyers helped me find the loopholes in the homestead provisions. Commutation is one of them. Relinquishment is another."

"They *had* to be in there," Hogan protested. "If a man can't make his land work for him, he can't just walk off and leave it lying there forever. There had to be a way to put it back in circulation."

"Sell it, you mean?"

"Sell his relinquishment, yes. So another man can have a try at it. It's not exactly selling the land, because he didn't own it yet. But the second man is under the same restrictions."

"Unless he wants to convert it with a pre-emption right—for a dollar and a quarter an acre. Then he's free to sell. So it all comes down to the same old scramble. The man with the money or the ideas winds up with all the good land."

"You got money?" Hogan challenged.

"I've got ideas." Vern sat straight on the seat, balancing himself, gripping the lines tightly. The horses were a couple of hundred yards behind now. "And I've got horses. That may be a tough combination to break."

"You can't win—not the big acreages you men want! Why spoil things for a lot of small farmers?"

"Maybe I'll go after townsites. Maybe a couple of square blocks of the new town of Pawnee would satisfy me."

"Oh, so that's—!" Hogan said.

Just then Vern released the reins and shouted at the horses. They broke instantly into a terrified run. He threw himself sidewise on the seat.

Hogan fell back on the lumpy tarpaulin. He had no gun—just a kingbolt he had picked up at the stable. Hogan shouted and tried to scramble to his knees. Vern knelt on the seat, getting his balance. As he dived onto Hogan, the boomer swung the kingbolt at his head. It connected solidly with his shoulder; his left arm was instantly paralyzed. He cocked and hit Hogan in the face with his fist, but Hogan was rolling aside. Hogan came up on his knees, the big, dark face distorted.

As Vern waded after him, he swung the kingbolt again. Vern caught his wrist and the bolt fell. He drove the edge of his fist into the man's big, hard chin. The shock was a clean-smacking sound and he could feel his wrist bend back with the force of it. Hogan sprawled loosely on the wagon-bed.

In the dusty night behind the wagon, horses could be heard running and a man shouted something. Holding onto the side of the wagon, Vern worked forward. Traffic had knocked ruts and potholes into the road, and the holes twisted at the wheels so that the wagon slewed from side to side. He could hear things falling onto the road, and it seemed to him that at any moment a wheel would drop into the bar-pit and the wagon would go over. The hot night wind blew against his face. He clutched the back of the seat and crawled over it. Then he had to grope for the lines, which were dangling in the clattering void between the horses. One by one, he fished them up. Then he eased back onto the seat and started taking the horses in.

The team fought him. He talked to them as he pulled back on the lines. He hoped he had hit Hogan hard enough to keep him under wraps for a while. Close behind the wagon, he heard horses running, and he turned his head to see three riders coming up through the dust. Suddenly he recognized Tom Trago, standing up in the stirrups with his weight well forward. Trago was flogging his horse with his hat. He brought the horse up head-to-head with the nigh horse of the team and leaned over to take hold of the bridle. Will Motley came up on the other side and they brought the team to a halt.

Trago was grinning. There were scabbed cuts on his mouth and eyebrow from his battle with Vern that morning. "You been gone too long, son," he said. "Used to could handle a team better than that."

Vern twisted to look behind him. He stared. There was no sign of Hogan.

"You lost a man back yonder," Trago said. "Slade dropped off to look for him. He crawled into the brush. What kind of freight you haulin' these days?"

"This was a stowaway—Dan Hogan!" Vern said.

"By the Lord!" Trago exclaimed. He stared across the wagon at Motley. "Will, we're gonna barbecue us a boomer! Can you handle that team now, Congressman? We're goin' back and make sure Slade don't lose us our man!" He pulled his rifle from the saddle-boot and put his horse over.

"Hey!" Vern yelled. But Trago waved the rifle and loped back down the road. Motley followed him at a jog.

Vern swore. He knew what Trago had in mind. Hogan would be lucky if Trago gave him a chance to surrender. He pulled off the road, set the brake and ran back to his saddle-horse. He found the bridle under the tarp and pushed the bit into the pony's mouth. Then he cut loose the lead-rope and mounted....

A half-mile back, he found Trago and the others working back and forth through a brushy thicket flanking the road. "Seen him crawl in here! That's for dang sure," Slade swore. He was using his rifle-barrel to move branches aside as he peered into the thicket.

Trago rode along the plowed field behind the thicket, flogging it with a coil of rope. "If he's still in there," he said, "we'll get him."

"Listen a minute—" Vern said.

Trago pulled up. "Boys!" he said sharply. He dropped his rope over his saddle-horn and dug into his coat pocket. "There's a better way than all this quarterin' around." He made a wiping motion, and a match fizzed into flame. "You tell me a better way to catch a boomer," he said, smiling at the match, "than to burn him out."

Vern made a pass at the match and the flame went out. Trago's glistening eyes came to him. "We going to have trouble over a boomer?" he asked quietly.

"We are if you try to be judge and jury. Hogan's going to jail alive. He's out of action—what more do you want?"

"I want him roasted and crawling," Trago said.

"If you want Hogan, you'll have to deal with me first."

Trago wiped his mouth. "Well—I reckon that can be managed," he said.

Vern snapped: "That stiff neck of yours is going to wind up in a rope, too. I came back here with a plan for us. It'll keep us in business. But if you kill Hogan, we're quits. I want no part of a Comanche war."

"When I need the help of a cub like you," said Trago, I hope they bury me quick."

"Let him talk, Tom," Will Motley said. "We came after him to hear what he had to say. Don't deny it. Now let's listen."

"You won't listen until Hogan's in jail," Farrell said. "Two days from now, if we don't have some kind of a plan, we're finished. No cows, no land, no money. You'd look good cadging drinks in a farmer-town, Tom."

Trago hesitated. He took another match from his pocket and looked at it. He struck it and let it burn nearly to his fingers before he puffed it out.

"You *better* have a plan, boy. You better had!" He shoved the rifle roughly into the boot. "All right, Hogan!" he shouted. "Come on out!"

Across the road there was a crackling of brush. A man crawled onto the road. He had obviously been listening to the debate. Trago spurred across the road and stared down at him. In a moment the man, who was obviously in pain, was surrounded by horsemen. He looked up at them, his face twisting.

"I think my ankle's broken," he said.

"That's a pity," jeered Trago. "Ain't that tough, boys? We're broke and out of business—but he's got a busted ankle! Excuse us if we don't break down, Hogan."

Hogan swore at him as he struggled to his knees. Vern dismounted to help him. "I'm not asking for sympathy! I'm just explaining why I can't get up and lick the tar out of you."

"Give me a hand with him," Vern said. "He can ride my horse into town. Bring the horse back after you've taken him in."

Trago nodded. "All right. We'll see him to jail. Then we'll be out to hear about these big doin's of yours."

CHAPTER 8

It was like old times in the Strip.

In the smoke and dust, seven men stood about the breakfast fire. The air was rich with the fragrances of coffee and bacon. Already the unseasonal autumn heat of this September of 'Ninety-three was setting in, while the earth gave back the warmth it had collected the day before. Gnats hovered in clouds about the horses grazing along the creek.

Trago and the others had come in during the night. They had slept on the ground beneath the wagon. They had eaten, and now it was time to talk business. Trago bit the end from a long cigar, lighted a little branch and held it to the cigar while he puffed. Then he dropped the branch and watched the yellow fuzz on the ground catch and blacken, but did nothing to stop it. This was a trick he had which Vern had almost forgotten. Just when it seemed about to get out of hand, he trod the fire out with his boot.

"You had a proposition, Mistuh Farrell," Trago said cheerfully.

Vern set down his coffee cup.

"Wait a minute," Trago said, putting a hard look on Vern's men, Bill Spence and Cole Johnson. "How come these fellows are sitting in?"

"They work for me. I'm cutting them in if they like the deal."

"What if they don't like it?" Trago argued. "They'll still know about it."

"They're bound to like it. They've already signed to ride for me, and who's going to turn down more money than he was guaranteed?"

Spence grinned, and Johnson said, "Can't hurt my feelings that way."

Trago looked at them closely, then shrugged and patted the leather shirt over his flat belly. "Go ahead."

"Well, it's in two parts: where we're going, and what we'll use for money to get there. Where we're going is Wyoming, Idaho, Arizona—anywhere there are government forest leases."

Trago lowered his cigar. "If backing out is all you've got to suggest—"

"Shut up," Old Man Cuff said. "Let him talk."

Trago narrowed his eyes and took the cigar again.

"Moving will be easy. All our cattle are sold and we never did have much equipment. But leases cost money, and so does a mother-herd. So we come to Part Two: raising money."

Tom Trago's black eyes were sour with displeasure. He was against the scheme before he had even heard it.

"I've got thirty horses down the creek," Vern continued. "I bought them in Kansas City for an average of thirty dollars a head. I'll sell them to you at cost—except for a fair share I'm holding for myself."

He stopped. Trago looked suspicious, but he did not interrupt.

"Getting riders won't be any problem. The town is full of cowpunchers looking for a way to make a dollar. Now we've got horses and riders: that brings us to the Opening. There may be a thousand men lined up to the mile. But only three men in this town know the area—Trago, Dan Hogan, and I. Hogan was in the original survey party, and he's poked around the Strip during the last year; but now we know he's not going to make the run. So Trago and I will be the only qualified guides in town."

A firelog snapped loudly; horses dragged their hobbles through the grass. The men were thoughtful.

"What we'll go after will be town-lots. A year from now, a lot in the middle of Pawnee will go for five or six thousand dollars! The government's picked the logical spot for a town this time. Pawnee's got water, level land, and a railroad already on the boards. We'll have all the best town-lots staked out before anybody else is in sight."

Trago spread his hands. "And who gets the money? The men who took the claims!"

"They'll get half the money." Vern smiled. "That's the deal we'll make before we sign them up for the Run. I've got papers drawn up, ready to sign."

Motley toed a branch farther into the fire. "Who's going to ride for half the money when he could ride his own horse for all of it?"

"What if he hasn't got a horse? I know plenty of cowpunchers who never rode anything but a company horse. A man who doesn't own a horse will have everything to gain and nothing to lose by riding for us."

Cuff shook his head. "It won't work. You can't sell a homestead till after five years. In five years we'll be clean out of the picture."

"A homesteader can convert his land and sell in fourteen months," Vern told him. "We can take our lots, pay a fee to clear them, and re-sell when we're ready."

Trago peered into the fire. "Are you trying to tell me that with a hundred thousand boomers waiting to take claims, nobody else is going to think of this?"

"They've got to do more than think of it, Tom," Farrell said. "They've got to know where they're going."

Trago rubbed his chin with his thumb. Motley made

one of his cattle-brands in the dirt with a stick. "What if we haven't got money to buy the horses?"

"I'll carry you."

"Maybe we'd do better to sell the horses to boomers," Cuff said practically.

Vern felt a nettle of resentment. "All right, do what you want with them, damn it! I'm keeping six for myself, and I'm going to make better than two thousand dollars out of each claim I take with them. It's up to you."

Motley took a chamois poke from his pocket and unclasped it. He took out some gold coins and counted them. "I'll take five of them horses," he said.

Cuff began to nod. "I'll get the money out of the bank today."

Trago held his cigar up like a pencil and watched the thin spiral of smoke rise in the quiet air. "It ain't what I'd call a big victory," he said. "Dragging your tail to Arizona because you were whipped in Oklahoma. But it may keep us in business. And while we stay in business, a lot of these farmers will be going broke. You run and hide if you want, but Trago's going to be raising cattle in the Strip when they bury the last boomer!"

Vern smiled. He offered his hand. Trago's grin came reluctantly. They shook hands, but to Vern's disappointment the rancher did not say, *I'm sorry about the fight;* he made no concession to humility. This was, Vern saw, a truce, not a peace.

They rode into town. More settlers had come in by wagon and stagecoach, a few more scraps of canvas had been tucked into the vast encampment in the middle of the town. The first move, Vern told them, was to get their own registration certificates at the government land office. There was a registration booth every few miles along the four-hundred-mile perimeter of the land which, at noon the day after tomorrow, would be invaded by four times as many frantic homesteaders as there were claims for.

Outside the land office in town, the line was a half-block long. It was an hour before they were inside the stifling little room near the *Warrior* office. Jeff Ridge was there, Hogan's worshipful shadow who had hit Farrell the day before. He was with a lawyer named Myron Tackett, who was Hogan's adviser. They were talking to some boomers in the line, and Vern heard the nervous, energetic Ridge tell them:

"Mr. Hogan's all right—don't worry about him. He'll be ready to ride when that cannon booms!"

Trago grinned at Vern. "Ready to ride, and ridin', ain't exactly the same thing."

Ridge turned quickly, but Tackett put a hand on his arm. Ridge looked at them then—Trago, Vern, Cuff and Motley—and smiled derisively.

"Looks like they've come to Jesus," he said. "Going to be farmers like all the other good people, eh?"

When no one answered him, he started to turn back. Then he glanced at someone who had just come through the crowded doorway into the room.

"There's that damned girl!" he muttered to Tackett.

Vern had just received his sealed certificate. He glanced around. Rachel, looking flushed but determined, had crowded into the room and was now coming to the counter where the four clerks were sweating at their ledgers, entering names and handing out certificates. She was carrying the large tapestry bag she had carried on the train, and her hand dipped into it and she pulled out a little packet of leaflets.

"Excuse me," she said to Vern, not recognizing him as she tried to push through to the counter. "May I just—?"

"You just help yourself." Vern smiled, and she knew his voice and gave him a quick, flustered smile. She asked the clerk:

"May I leave these with you? I'd be much obliged if you'd hand one out with each certificate."

"What are they?" the clerk asked. He was a sour-eyed old man with a large, naked-looking nose. He glanced at the leaflets and shook his head. "This is a government land office. I can't be handing out propaganda, ma'am. You should know that."

"Suppose I just leave them here, then, and the customers can help themselves if they care to?"

"Go ahead." The clerk smirked. "Don't know why anybody'd want to take away the only comfort most of them will have this winter, with no crop put by and nothing to live on—"

"I don't know how you can call liquor a *comfort*," Rachel said, "when—"

"I'll take one of them, ma'am," said Bill Spence generously.

"Thank you," Rachel said, giving him that wonderful smile she saved for special people. Then she said, "If you don't mind—" She was pulling another packet of tracts from the bag. "Would you leave some of these at each of the saloons? I can't very well go in myself, and I *would* like—"

Vern told him drily, "Watch yourself, Bill. I'm not so sure you're the man for the job—"

Spence looked uncomfortable.

"Now, I'm sure you aren't afraid of public opinion—?" Rachel chided the cowboy, and Spence let her put the leaflets in his hand.

"Well—" he said.

And now he had the tracts and she was saying with an engaging smile, "Thank you *so* much. You've very kind." She left before he could lay hand to any more excuses.

Vern told Trago and the others he would be seeing them later, and hurried after her. He caught up with her just before she reached the *Warrior* office. Walking behind her, he liked the provocative swing of her long skirts, the slenderness of her waist. She was too attractive a girl to be dedicating her life to an abstract and unrewarding thing like handing out tracts, he thought.

She glanced uneasily from the corner of her eye as he came abreast of her, then recognized him and looked relieved. Glancing at the envelope in his hand, she said:

"I see you're making plans for the Run, Mr. Farrell. Are you planning to run cattle on a hundred and sixty acres?"

"You never know what you'll be forced to do," Vern said. "I don't expect Spence ever thought he'd be handing out temperance tracts in saloons."

Rachel frowned.

"Is that—is he the man you told me about?"

"That's him. He says he's taken the pledge. Though I don't take much stock in overnight reformations." He looked out over the square, from which dust and smoke rose like the palpable exhalations of wretchedness, and he said significantly: "Any more than I look for a miracle to be passed by putting people like that on land that can't be farmed." He shuddered. "Look at them! How do they live in a hog-wallow like that?"

Rachel spoke impatiently. "You're really a very unrealistic man. For most of those people that camp is an *improvement!* You haven't seen a real tenement in an Eastern city, have you...no a Southern farm that had been farmed out—whipped until it didn't have another blade of grass in it? *That's* what you've got to think about when you feel sorry for them. But as for feeling sorry for a few cattlemen—"

"What about the settlers who don't get claims? Aren't you going to feel sorry for them?"

Rachel sighed. "Well, if one out of ten of them gets a homestead, I suppose it would be worthwhile."

"Not to the other nine," Vern said. "Or to me."

They went into the shop. Fred, the printer, was setting up type from a paper hanging on a clip before him. There was a tumbler of lemonade in his hand, which he was just lowering. Wiping his mouth, he glanced sheepishly at Vern.

"'Tain't bad," he said.

"It looks pretty good," Vern said. In fact, it looked better than most lemonade, and while Rachel poured two more glasses from a pitcher he took a sip of the printer's drink. It had been laced to the lemonseeds with whisky. "Better than that rotten stuff most printers drink," he said solemnly.

Rachel handed a glass to him. He noticed her smooth,

thin fingers on the glass, and managed to touch them as he accepted it. The impropriety was not lost on her. She glanced down and picked up her glass. Vern raised his in a toast.

"To temperance," he said. "May the sound of hiccups never be heard in Oklahoma."

They sipped the cool drink. Rachel patted her brow with a handkerchief. "It's cooler in back, I think. We get a little breeze there."

They passed through the curtain. In the back room there was a press, a boiler with rusty fittings, a big paper-cutter, a table, and a stove. The whole rear wall was screened. A door opened onto another room.

"My bedroom," Rachel said. "Now that my father doesn't require it. . . ."

"Did you hear about last night?"

Sitting on a straight-back chair, she looked at her lemonade. "Yes. He was so foolish. I'm sorry he caused you trouble. You knew his ankle was broken?"

"He's lucky he wasn't shot. Trago's a rough playmate."

He saw a little pile of books, with some other things which seemed to have been recently unpacked—a silver hairbrush, a little china receptacle for loose hairs combed out of the brush, and some other things which obviously had not been the property of Daniel Hogan. He glanced at one of the titles. It was a book on economics by Adam Smith. There was another book called *The Rights of Property in England*, and a book on woman suffrage. Not surprisingly, there was a volume on the experiences of a temperance worker in a big Eastern city.

"Do you always think big thoughts?" he asked her.

"Big thoughts?" she parried.

"Like taking whisky from men and giving votes to women."

Rachel ran her finger around the rim of her glass; but it was too thick to sing. "I have my more trifling moments," she hinted.

Vern leaned toward her. "Do you ever think about men

and women—as such—when you're being trifling?" he asked.

She looked up, fearful of getting into something improper. "I don't—know what you mean."

He smiled. "Sometimes I think you're just shy, Rachel. I think big thoughts keep you from being confused by little thoughts—like men and women."

She gave a nervous laugh. "I don't think that's so little."

"It really isn't, when you come down to it." There was pink in her cheeks, and she had sounded breathless when she laughed. He put his hand out and touched the smooth skin of the back of her hand. She stiffened, but seemed too paralyzed to move.

"Like the way your skin is like satin, and mine is like cowhide. You can hardly see the pores in your skin. Isn't that remarkable? And did you ever notice the difference in men and women's voices? I used to come into Fort Smith after a year on the range, and the first thing I'd notice would be the women's voices. It was always surprising. I used to think a man's voice was like burlap, and a woman's was like silk. I'd think about that when I went back again...."

Rachel looked up at him, her eyes timid but her expression that of a woman who has made up her mind to be bold. "Those aren't little thoughts. Those are very big ones. They're much too big for high noon. So if..."

"I know," he said softly. "I was just seeing whether you knew the difference. You passed the test. And I'm going to give you a little prize now...."

Leaning forward, he was able to bring his face up to hers. She leaned back quickly, but the straight-backed chair kept her from retreating very far. He touched his mouth to hers, and there was such surprising softness and warmth in her lips that he experienced a pleasant shock. Then she put her hand on his chest, and he sat back. He smiled. She was so indignant she was unable to speak. He stood up.

"I shouldn't have stayed so long," he said. "I guess I'd better go."

"Well, I guess you had!" she exclaimed. "What made you think you could—?"

"I'm sorry," he said. "I didn't think I could anything. I just had to find out. Just another of the things that make a man different from a woman, you see."

She remained seated there, her glass clenched in both hands, while he walked to the door. He glanced back with a frown, hesitating. He wondered whether she was really angry. He hoped she was not, because he was begining to want to know her better, to know how she felt about a great many things; what she liked to do for amusement. It might be appropriate to give her some little present by way of apology, if he had really been out of line. Or, he wondered, did he just want to give her something to know that it would be near her—as his proxy, so to speak?

"Thank you for the lemonade," he said. "And good luck to you and your boomers."

Still looking down at her lap, she murmured, "Thank you."

Feeling guilty, and bothered by the implications of these sudden feelings about her, he went out.

CHAPTER 9

Jeff Ridge was watching when the ugly little cowboy named Bill Spence came from the Cherokee Bar. Spence appeared to have disposed of some of the temperance tracts he had promised Rachel Grant to leave at the saloons, and now he came along the walk toward Ridge frowning like a man who wished he was doing something else.

Ridge had been busy since he left the land office. Seeing the ranch crowd getting registration certificates—their passports to the Cherokee Strip day after tomorrow—he and Tackett, the lawyer, knew they were up to something. But Tackett couldn't guess what it was.

"No matter how you swing that cat," he said, "it comes to the same thing: there's one claim to a customer."

"Now, you know they ain't about to settle for a quarter-section," Ridge snapped. He was a sensitive, moody man whose main fault was taking everything personally. He was less *for* free land than he was *against*

69

cattlemen and Indians. The arrogance of the cow-crowd
enraged him. He burned with a fierce hatred of Vernon
Farrell and Tom Trago for having brought the Grant
woman to Oklahoma to cripple Dan Hogan's efforts to
put the right men on the right claims. Ridge had been
grinding a special ax of his own when Rachel Grant
stopped everything. He had rendered devoted service to
Dan Hogan, and had been promised a town-lot in return
for it.

"Maybe they're going after a string of adjoining
claims," the lawyer mused. "Try to block off the
railroad—something like that...."

"Hell, you don't know no more about it than I do,"
Ridge retorted. "I'm going to talk to Hogan."

"Why upset him with rumors?" Tackett protested.
"He's feeling low enough as it is."

But Ridge walked up to the jail and got permission to
visit Hogan in his cell. The big man looked tired. He had
skinned his face when he fell off the wagon the previous
night, and his broken ankle had been splinted. He looked
ill. "How are things, Jeff?" he asked wearily.

"Not so good, Dan. They're taking out registration
certificates."

"Who? Farrell's crowd?" Hogan looked disturbed.

Ridge hunched on the cell cot beside him, squeezing his
hands together. He nodded. "What good's a quarter-
section going to do them?"

"Farrell said something about town-lots," Hogan
muttered. "I don't know whether he was bluffing or not.
But there *are* ways they could dispose of any claims they
took for cash."

"I reckon one apiece wouldn't make much of a dent—"

"Unless one apiece isn't all they've got in mind. If we
just knew, we could make plans."

Suddenly a beam of light slanted into Jeff Ridge's
mind. "I'll find out."

"How?"

Smiling mysteriously, Jeff Ridge walked from the jail.
Standing now in the hot sun, he raised his hand to stop

Bill Spence from passing him. He smiled. Ridge had a clean, hard, man's-man smile when he wanted to turn it on. It worked wonderfully on women and almost as well on men.

"What've you got, cowboy—maps?"

Spence did not seem to remember him from the land office. He handed him a tract. Ridge fell in step as he went up the scooped-out dirt walk.

"*Would You Sell Your Soul for a Drink of Whisky?*" he read aloud, and chuckled. "No, but I might for a glass of cold beer."

He saw the cowboy swallow. As they reached Lund's Saloon, Spence started to enter.

"Hey, now—you're not going into that there den of iniquity, are you?" Ridge joked.

"I've got to get rid of these things," Spence growled.

Grinning, Ridge followed him inside. Spence went quickly to the end of the bar and placed the remainder of the leaflets on the mahogany. A bartender came up to take his order. He frowned at the tracts as Spence started away.

"Hey!" he called angrily after him. "You can't leave this stuff here. What's the matter with you?" He pushed them onto the floor.

Ridge stepped in the cowboy's path to prevent his leaving. "Pick them up," he said quietly to the bartender.

"*You* pick them up, if you want them," the bartender retorted. He was a tall man with waxed mustaches. His long white apron was stained about the midriff where he wiped his hands.

Ridge was big in the shoulders, with thick, muscular arms. He reached over the bar and pulled the bartender up close. He said again, as quietly as before: "Pick-them-up." The violence in Ridge's eyes gleamed through. The barman started to raise his hand. "*Ah* right—what the hell!" he muttered.

Coming around the end of the bar, he gathered the leaflets and replaced them. He went back and stared flatly at Ridge. "Anything else?"

"A boilermaker." Ridge laid his hand on Bill Spence's shoulder. "What's yours?"

"I'm not taking anything right now," Spence said. "I tied one on in K.C. that'll last me a spell."

"A sa's'parilla, maybe? Bartender, a sa's'parilla for my friend," Ridge said.

When the drinks came, Ridge salted down the foam on his beer, drank the whisky, and followed it with the beer chaser. He blew out his cheeks and smiled dreamily at Spence, who had tasted the soft drink and set it down.

"Man, that does it. Great Snakes, but it's hot!" Ridge said. "I swear beer must have been invented on a day like this.—Let's have another," he told the barman.

The second beer he drank in one long, smooth, eyes-closed draft. "Wish you'd have one," he said.

"Well—maybe just a beer," Spence said.

"That's the stuff. There's nothing like it." He ordered Spence's beer and a third for himself, but when the drinks arrived he pushed his untasted whisky over to Spence with a careless gesture.

"You'd better have this. I've had my quota of hard liquor."

Spence picked it up and held it between two fingers for a full fifteen seconds, testing his strength. He grinned.

"Take the taste of that sa's'parilla out of my mouth," he said. He put it down as quickly and neatly as throwing it out. His face screwed up with shock and he quickly drank half the beer. "Yes, sir," he said, "that does it . . . !"

Early that evening the two friends parted. Spence had shown his sealed registration certificate and confided a secret which he emphasized must not go any farther. He was being hired to take a claim for Farrell. Ridge promised to keep it to himself. But he grew suddenly restless.

"Maybe you ought to be getting back to camp," he said.

Spence heaved with silent laughter. "You know what? What'm gonna do? Get some more uh them temp'rance tracks from Miss—Miss What's-'er-name—"

"Grant," smiled Ridge.

"That's it," said Spence, starting for the office of the *Oklahoma Warrior*.

"Attaboy," said Ridge.

With Spence gone into the languid night crowds of the walk, Ridge turned and strode across the street to plunge into the big murmuring tent city. There was a soft radiation of firelight from the whole encampment, a luminescence of lanterns and fires spread by the dust, so that the camp pulsated light in the same way that a lightning-bug glowed. Ridge was looking for a small brown pup-tent, old-army issue, but when he found it, it was deserted. From nearby came the wheezing nostalgia of a concertina, and men and women singing *In the Gloaming*.

Ridge threaded tent-ropes, boxes, and buckets, and worked along behind lines of tied horses to find the campfire. It was a small fire, the night being already too hot; a fire just big enough to keep a blackened coffee-pot bubbling, and around it were gathered the homesteaders. Across the fire he saw a man with a thin hard face and red cavalry mustaches. He had a chin like a saddlehorn and his sandy hair grew forward in a brush. His name was Dick Sullivan. Ridge signaled to him. Sullivan had worked on railroads, in livery stables, on farms, and in saloons. He had sharp vixen features, with something wary in them. Sullivan left the fire and joined him.

"What's the uproar?" he asked.

"I'm going to play a Hallowe'en trick on somebody tonight," Ridge murmured. "Where's your horse, Sully?"

"Mite early for Hallowe'en."

"Early, nothing. I've only got twenty-four hours. Where's your horse?"

"Yonder. What's the pay?"

Ridge punched him. "Greedy cuss. Twenty dollars."

He had the double-eagle ready, and dropped it in Sully's hand. "Now?" the smaller man asked.

Ridge nodded. "I'll get my horse and meet you in front of the Cherokee."

"What are we going to do?"

"Chouse a few horses around. Nothin' to it."

"Wait a minute," Sully said. "They hang horse-thieves in Oklahoma."

"We're not going to steal them. Just run them a ways.... Far enough so's the owners will be a week collecting them again."

CHAPTER 10

Bill Spence was asleep now, snoring loudly and occasionally moaning on his blanket under a tree. Vern and Trago had found him in one of the saloons and gotten him back to camp on a horse.

"Be a miracle if I get him boiled out in time for the Run," Farrell mourned. There were fifteen men among the trees—cowboys pledged to make the Run for the Association ranchers. He pulled a boot off and stood it beside the tarpaulin on which his saddle and gear lay. This was all that vows and temperance tracts would ever accomplish for men like Spence. The only salvation for him was to work on a ranch forty miles from town, just as the only hope of long life for a stick of dynamite was to stay away from fires. He was beginning to like the little cowpuncher and he wished he had a place to send him right now.

He lay down, with a deep, end-of-the-day sigh. Then he heard the horses.

At first he thought one had stumbled and frightened the herd. A moment later he heard the trampling clatter of the whole herd moving along the creek. He sat up quickly. Everyone was rolling out, and Trago, like a night animal, was already on his feet in the dark, his Colt in his hand.

"What the hell goes on?" he snarled.

Vern pulled on his boots. Only one man was with the horses. One guard seemed enough, all the graze and water being along the creek, so that there was nothing to tempt the animals to stray.

"Who's with the horses?" Trago bawled.

"Johnson," Vern replied. "Funny—I don't hear any hobbles!"

"That son of a homesteader has sold us out!" Trago shouted.

He ran to his horse, in the remuda among the trees. Vern bitted up his pony but did not take time to saddle. He took his rifle from the wagon and mounted. Trago had already taken off after the horses. The night was black. Far to the north the lights of the town glowed against the sky. The rattling of hoofs had moved north and spread over a wider area. Vern rode through the dark, trying to follow the sounds, but it was several minutes before he saw one of the horses. When he tried to work it back toward the creek it broke into a run. For an instant it was silhouetted against the town-glow; with a start, he saw that the horse had a rider.

"Hold it!" he shouted.

A dull red explosion and a blast of sound stunned him. Something went by his head like a nighthawk. He raised his rifle and fired. A man cried out. He heard him hit the ground. The horse ran on. Vern reined in and listened. He worked the loading lever of the rifle and pointed it at where the rider had fallen. He could hear him groaning. Far off he heard horses running. They were heading toward town now, and he thought of all the boomer camps in the fields where horse-hungry men might capture a stray horse and forget where they had found him.

He dismounted behind his horse and watched until he could see the man he had wounded. He was sitting on the ground, rocking back and forth. Vern worked in closer to him and finally saw a Colt lying on the earth several feet away. He seemed to be in a state of shock, so that when Vern walked up and took the revolver he hardly looked up. Shoving the gun under his belt, Vern stared at him. He did not recognize the man. It was quiet where they were; the noise of moving horses was out of earshot. The rider had lost his hat. His features looked thin and wolfish and he wore a reddish cavalry-style mustache.

"What's your name?" Vern asked. The man looked up. He seemed to be coming out of his stupor.

"I'm hit," he said numbly.

Vern squatted near him. "Where are you hit?"

The man touched his collar-bone. There was blood on his shirt. "Who were you with?" Vern asked him.

Shaking his head slowly, the other said, "Never seen him before."

Vern rose and stepped back. "Get on your feet, boy. You may see him again. We're going back to camp."

At the horse-camp, a lantern had been hung from the side of the wagon. Someone had built the fire up. The men were staring at a man spread-eagled with his back to a wheel of the wagon. Trago was standing before him with his hands on his hips. In the firelight, Vern recognized Hogan's man, Jeff Ridge, with whom he had tangled in the Cherokee Bar. A lot of skin was missing from one side of the boomer's face. Trago held a coil of rope in one hand.

"Who sent you?" Trago was asking him.

"Tom!" Farrell called. "We've got another."

Trago turned and looked at the man stumbling into the light ahead of Farrell's horse. "Gannies!" he chuckled. "They're crawlin' out of the brush. Our man's horse took a fall. Looks like you winged yours."

Vern swung down and pulled the man up to the fire. He ripped his shirt open to look at his wound. Across the muscle sloping from the base of his neck to his shoulder was a bloody slash almost like a rope-burn.

"He'll live to hang," Trago said.

Vern glanced at him. "Let me have your whisky," he said.

Trago uncorked the liquor and handed it to him. Vern let the red-haired man drink from the bottle. Then he tore off part of the man's shirt-tail, soaked it with whisky, and slapped it on the wound. The man groaned through his teeth.

"Who sent you?" Vern asked him.

"Nobody."

"What's your name?"

"Dick Sullivan."

Vern glanced around at the cowboys who had drifted in to stare at Sullivan. "Anybody know him?"

"I've seen him," Will Motley muttered.

"Do you work for Hogan?"

"Leave him be," Jeff Ridge growled. "He was with me. I just wanted to stir things up a little."

Vern saw Cole Johnson standing nearby. "Where were you all this time?" he asked Johnson.

Johnson shook his head. "I was with the horses. I guess I wasn't paying much attention. They've stayed on the creek ever since we put them there."

"But somebody took off their hobbles before they were stampeded. Who?"

Johnson's dark, pitted face was stolid. "I don't know. I must've been asleep in the saddle. All I know is I heard 'em running."

"How many did we get back?"

"Four, so far. Only twenty-six missing," Trago said in irony.

Vern walked over to Ridge and stared into his dark, bloody face. "Whose idea was it?"

"Mine. Sully was just along for the ride."

"How much was Hogan paying you?"

"Told you it was my idea."

"You'll wish it was his before we're through," Vern said.

He poured himself a cup of coffee and added whisky. Through it all, beneath the wagon, Bill Spence had slept the deep and innocent sleep of a child. Johnson stood awkwardly near Vern.

"I'm sorry," he said. "My fault. I was just dead beat, that's all."

Vern didn't reply.

"Those horses," Trago said bitterly, "are probably across the Kansas line by now. What brand were they wearing?"

"The original brands," Vern said, "plus a road brand. The horses wouldn't run far. Somebody'd be bound to catch them anyway. That's assuming there weren't other men with these two who'd hide the critters somewhere."

"I told you we were just running them," Ridge said stolidly.

Trago laughed. He sounded almost as pleased as though they had recovered the horses. "Then we'll just use a running slip-knot around your necks when we hang you."

Farrell glanced at him. Trago had hung more than one man in his day, but the sun had gone down on that day. Whatever name was put on these men's crime, their punishment was a matter for the law.

Sullivan's red, fox-sharp features turned up quickly. "You can't hang a man for runnin' horses! We never stole any—didn't aim to—"

Thoughtfully, Earl Slade said, "We'd need a right heavy rope to do a proper job, Tom. . . ."

Trago slouched over and laid his hand appraisingly on Sullivan's shoulder. The boomer emitted a snarl like an animal and tried to stand up. Trago struck him behind the ear with his fist. The man went down, stunned.

Vern spoke firmly. "Slow down, now. Let's not talk about hanging until we know whether we're going to get the horses back. I want to know who else was in on this that might be holding them now."

"There weren't any others," Ridge repeated. "There was just him and me. I—I'll get them back for you."

Trago laughed. "You ain't in a position to get nothing back."

"I would be if you let us go," Ridge said, and Vern could feel him holding his breath. Standing spread-eagled against the wagon-wheel, he gazed out at them.

Trago stretched his chin with his thumb. "Well, why don't we?" he said suddenly. Walking to the wagon, he pulled a knife from his pocket and cut the pigging-strings with which Ridge had been tied. As the cords fell, Ridge began rubbing his wrists. He stared around the fire. He was afraid to move, fearing the next part of the joke would be sprung.

"Do we get our saddle-horses?"

Trago winked at Vern. "Sure—you get *your* horse."

"I—I reckon Sully can ride," Ridge said.

"Oh, no—we wouldn't want him ridin'," said Trago seriously. "He might sicken and we'd be blamed. We'll keep him here. *You* go get the horses."

"We'll take them both to jail," Vern put in curtly.

"Couldn't do that. Marshal Welty's a boomer himself. We want justice, don't we? This is a big, tame country where everything's done according to law—range law, where it touches on range crimes. Maybe Ridge'll round up the horses and bring them back by tomorrow night. But in case he don't show up—we hang Sullivan. Just like any other horse-thief."

The broken edge of the joke turned raggedly in Jeff Ridge. Clenching his hands, he gazed at the cattlemen about the fire. Then he looked at Trago, and with a sudden distortion of his face he shouted:

"The hell you will! He's goin' with me!"

He started toward the fire, but Trago put the knife-point in his belly. "Seems to me it's a pretty square deal we're offerin' you," he said. "We *could* hang you both."

Vern was not sure whether Trago meant it or not. But he did see one thing: they had the best leverage possible for getting the horses back.

"You'd better take it before the offer's withdrawn," he told Ridge. "It's a better deal than Sullivan was offering when he took a shot at me."

"I was just trying to scare you," Sullivan muttered.

"Bring Mr. Ridge's horse," Trago said.

Johnson led the horse up. It was limping from the fall in which Jeff Ridge had been captured. "Git aboard," Trago said. Ridge suddenly walked over and leaned down to squeeze his friend's arm.

"Don't worry, Sully—they know we'd hunt 'em down like jackrabbits if they hurt you. I'll bring the horses back and have you out of here before tomorrow night."

As the boomer mounted, Trago stood with his hands shoved into his hip-pockets, watching him. "Don't think this is a bluff, mister," he said. "There's only one way Sullivan leaves here if those horses don't come back—in a box!"

Ridge's gaze traveled the circle of faces. Then he swung his horse suddenly and rode off.

Rubbing his hands together, Trago stood staring down at Sullivan. Vern watched him. "Tom," he said finally. Trago looked around, and Vern walked a few yards away. Trago followed him. "It *is* a bluff—let's have that understood," Vern said pointedly.

"Bluff, hell!" rapped Trago. "We get the horses, or Sullivan's neck gets stretched."

"Are you crazy? Ridge was telling it straight: if we lynch Sullivan, they'll hunt us down man by man and hang us too. It's their country—not ours."

Trago spat. "It's theirs if we hand it to 'em! But by God, here's one cowman that ain't afraid to fight!"

"Fine," Vern snapped. "You make your fight. But not with our necks. Leave Sullivan alone."

Trago looked him over contemptuously. "Or maybe you've turned woman on us—is that it? You're afraid to

see him kickin' at the end of a rope. Well, don't you forget
something: we're at the end of a rope, too. And Sullivan's
breed put us there."

He turned his back and walked to the campfire.

CHAPTER 11

When Vern awoke the next morning, the boomer named Dick Sullivan had disappeared.

Near the fire, a tin cup of coffee at his side, Bill Spence was sitting on the ground with his head in his hands, badly hung over. Vern went looking for Trago, but his horse was gone from the rope stretched between two big pecan trees. He found Slade taking a can of sardines from a crate of supplies on the wagon.

"Where's Trago?" Vern demanded.

Slade looked at him, his long, windburned face faintly amused. "Ain't he around?"

"No. Did he take Sullivan somewhere?"

"Beats me," said Slade.

"Where are you taking the food?"

Slade regarded him lazily. "We may be all day tracking those horses. I don't aim to hunt horses on an empty stomach."

Other men were saddling and riding out to hunt the

horses. Spence got himself another cup of coffee and sat down again.

"Mister Farrell," he said weakly, "I'll be ridin' out direckly. But I reckoned I'd have a little of this here coffee first."

Vern told him to suit himself. He turned away to saddle his horse, but Spence said low, "Trago took that red-headed feller down the creek."

"Thanks."

Vern rode a mile down the creek without seeing anything but the mingled tracks of the horse-herd. Then he heard a man riding through the brush. He reined in and waited. Trago came into view. He smiled when he saw Vern, and halted his horse.

"Well, we lost out 'coon," he said resignedly.

"Where'd you hide him?"

"Hide him?" said Trago.

Vern seized the front of his shirt. "Yes, damn it! One of the men saw you taking him away."

"Well, now, I don't see how that can be. I was out early hunting horses, but I ain't seen anything of Sullivan."

He touched spurs to his horse and jogged on. Frustrated, Vern followed him back to camp. When they rode in, Jeff Ridge was there. He had brought some of the horses with him. Ridge walked stiffly to Vern and Trago at the line of saddle-horses and watched them dismount. One side of his face was swollen and striped with scabs.

"I brought back five of your horses," he said tensely. "I'll have the rest before dark. Where's Sully?"

Trago loosened the cinch of his saddle. "Done flew the coop, I reckon. Thought he'd gone back to town. Ain't you seen him?"

"By God, nothing had better happen to him!" Ridge choked.

"Nothin's gonna happen to him, if we get our horses."

Vern glanced away as Ridge turned to him. He did not know what to say to him. He was convinced that Trago had left the boomer tied somewhere, and that he meant to hang him if he was given the excuse. But there was nothing he could say to Ridge that would not be incriminating to himself if anything happened to Sullivan.

After a moment Ridge turned away and walked to his horse.

In an hour and a half he was back with Marshal Welty and six angry-eyed townsmen. Welty's big, square head turned as he searched the camp.

"Where's Sullivan?" he demanded angrily.

Vern was saddling a fresh horse. "I haven't seen him since last night."

Angrily, Welty stared about. "Where's Tom Trago?"

"Out hunting horses."

Welty leveled his arm at him. "Now you listen to me! You have Sullivan in my office by sundown, or I'm coming out here and take you in for kidnaping."

"I can't tell you where Sullivan is, marshal. Maybe he got hurt in a horse-fall. There's hazards in all trades— especially horse-stealing."

Welty quieted himself down. Ridge had been listening nervously. "All right," Welty said stolidly. "I know what went on. I've given Ridge hell, and I'll raise some hell with Sullivan when I get my hands on him. But if he's killed, I'll have the whole bunch of you in jail for murder."

"Not without evidence."

"We've got evidence. You threatened last night to hang him—that's evidence."

"That was Trago. I'll give you boys some advice: find Trago and lock him up until you find Sullivan. Trago's the fire-eater in this crowd."

"I don't care who eats the fire—you'll all get the bellyache if that man's hurt. That's a promise!"

The day's heat increased. Along the creek there was a rich odor of rot leaves, a humming of flies and gnats. Four more horses were brought in, raising the total to thirteen. Motley came back from town, where he had gone through the stables with the men he had hired to ride for him. They had found no horses, and the newly hired riders had quit and stayed in town. All the new men had now disappeared.

It was early afternoon. Vern glanced at the sun, relentlessly swinging down from its zenith. He watched Motley saunter to the water-bags and slake his thirst. Motley wiped his mouth and shook his head.

"Them horses could be in Kansas by now. Just wastin' our time."

Vern glanced narrowly at him. Then he asked quietly, "Will, where's Trago?"

"Ain't he back yet?" Motley asked innocently.

"You know he isn't."

"That's peculiar. Swore I saw him in town this morning."

Just then Tom Trago rode into camp.

Trago was swinging a rope and whistling as he came in. Vern watched him jog to the line of horses, tie his pony, and dump the saddle on the ground. He shook out the wet saddle-blanket and said to himself:

"Hooo-ee! Hot!" He opened his clasp knife and prepared to remove a stone from the horse's hoof.

Vern walked up and turned him by the shoulder. "Damn you, where is he?"

Trago had not shaved for two days and his coppery face was scarred and venomous, made harder by a cold and acrimonious strength of will. "I ain't his keeper," he drawled.

"We're all his keepers. We'll hang if he hangs, go free if we free him."

Trago glanced scornfully around at the men who were listening without seeming to listen. "I'd hate to think," he said, "that a cowman wasn't the match for a boomer shaking a rope in his face."

"How about a hundred boomers? Suppose they came after us?"

Trago slapped his hand significantly over his Colt and looked at him.

Vern snorted. "They won't come with pitchforks and

singletrees—they'll be carrying guns too!"

Trago tapped his shoulder. "If you want to scare me, talk about trying to raise cattle without land. Talk about fenced-off springs and cornfields. We went into this fight with a pretty fair shake to save our skins. Those horses were going to buy us another chance. Well, Sullivan helped dynamite that chance. If we don't get the horses back, we're finished. Now, mister, don't shake the tambourine under my nose and try to take up no collection for Dick Sullivan! I just ain't buying."

He tried to turn away, but Vern held his arm. "Tom, every word you say is true. He deserves killing—he and Ridge both. But we're not the ones to kill them. And if we do—they'll kill us. That's all I'm trying to tell you."

Trago smiled secretly and gazed around the camp, and said, "They ain't killed the Doolin boys. They ain't killed the Jameses."

Vern looked into the glinting black eyes, beginning to see into his mind now. "So that's what you're lining up for us! A gang of night-riders. Is that the kind of fight we're going to make?"

Under his stare, Trago shrugged. "I didn't say that. All I say is, guts will still buy a man a hand in any game he wants to set in." He walked over and picked up a dry saddle-blanket and dropped it over a fresh mount.

"That's a game I don't want to hold cards in, Tom," Vern said quietly.

"Nobody's asking you to. But if you really want to save Sullivan's neck, you'd better git out there and hunt horses."

Riding out through the camp, Trago stopped to stare fiercely at the men who were now killing time, waiting it out, having given up on finding the horses. Of the men who had been hired yesterday, not a rider was left.

"Well, ain't you got anything better to do than lay around scratching your bellies?" Trago said scornfully. "There's barns within two miles of here we haven't even looked into yet."

The men got up and wearily drifted toward the horses.

Vern shook his head and walked over to finish his coffee.

Tom Trago took his time riding away.

He thought ahead to what had to be done tonight. The first thing that had to be done was to unload the gun that was pointed at his head, and the gun was Farrell. When Trago was out of sight of the camp, he pulled into a tangle of brush to wait. In a short time he heard horses on the move, and saw the men one by one riding out across the rolling farmlands. He did not see Farrell. He was pleased. Things might be working out well.

Trago removed his spurs and stole quietly back to camp afoot. Moving through the thickets beside the creek, he watched for Farrell. Suddenly he saw him. Farrell was currying his horse preparatory to saddling. He had his back to Trago and there was about fifty feet between them.

Trago waited until he finished the currying and picked up his blanket and saddle. Then, moving like an Indian, he stepped from cover and started across the clearing. A mixed emotion stirred in Tom Trago. He had always liked Farrell. He had taught him things about survival in the wilderness that only the old-timers knew. In a way he had shaped him in his own image, giving him his pride and strength of spirit. He had thought he could predict what he would do in any situation. But then the locusts came to the land, and when it was time to fight, to make them feel your iron, Farrell had started finding excuses to crawfish.

Trago was halfway across the clearing, and as yet Farrell had not seen him. He had dropped the saddle on the horse and was reaching underneath it to grope for the off-strap. Drawing his gun, the rancher kept walking toward him quietly, toe and heel, like a prowling Sioux.

A sour resentment was in him, like the taste in one's mouth the morning after a drinking bout. Farrell could have been a help to him instead of a hindrance—his lieutenant in the little army of cowmen he had talked up with Motley and Cuff and Slade and some of the other cowmen he could trust. They had talked of raiding across the Strip—burning crops and barns, scattering livestock, making it plain that this was still cow-country. They had talked for months about it, and Trago had pictured the boomers giving up, one by one, and dragging out of the Strip with their knock-kneed wagons and underfed horses.

But Farrell had bucked him all the way, until at last Trago had decided to make his fight alone. He had finished in prison. He had failed to achieve the victory that a small, tough band of riders could have had.

And while he rotted in their stinking jail, Farrell had kept on with his soft-handed foolishness about a Territory of Cimarron set aside for cattlemen. From the first, Trago had known it would never be accepted. Now the sham-fighting was all over, and it was time to draw the knife and go to war.

Suddenly Farrell heard him and turned his head. His mouth dropped open; he tried to duck. But Trago lunged in with his raised pistol and brought the gunbarrel down like a tomahawk. The blued steel caved in the crown of his Stetson and bit into his scalp. He went to his knees as the horse shied. Dropping to one knee beside him, Trago waited to see whether he was finished. He felt a stab of remorse as Farrell went slack and stretched out on the ground.

Slowly Trago rose. He looked down in remorse. But it had had to be done; just as the other thing had to be done, too, and a soft hand could not be allowed to prevent it. Trago shoved his gun into the holster and walked back to where he had left his horse.

CHAPTER 12

In Trago's mind, burning like a fiery cross on a hill, was the dream of hanging Dick Sullivan. For into Sullivan had been packed all the guilt of every homesteader Trago had ever hated. All the poor, dirt-sifting, hangdog lot of them.

He was the model from which the whole graveyard full of statues had been copied. He was the whiner, the swaggerer, the failure, who weighed less than a bluejay's feather alone, but could crush and suffocate in the mass. He was the spoiler of the open range, the thief of something he could not use when he had stolen it.

After riding about two miles downstream, Tom Trago waited for dark, slapping at mosquitoes and blowing cigar-smoke at gnats. The rusty twilight deepening, he rode from the woods along the creek into a field of broom-corn which had not been worked for a full year. Disreputable shocks of blackening cornstalks reeled across the land like drunken soldiers in formation. The horse's hoofs rang on the baked, alligatored soil.

Trago came to the edge of a clearing.

In the dusk, the signature had almost faded of the settler who had jumped breathless from his horse on this spot, to pound his stake and raise his arms like a victorious rodeo-rider. Having won the race, he had lived to go broke on the land that loved cattle and wild things, but lay like a frightened bride under the hands of the homesteader. Other homesteaders had scavenged his equipment. Only a lean-to shed and a sod-house were left. Rain and wind had sluiced away at the sod-house. The back of it was caved in, and the roof was a long weedy ramp rising from the ground. At the front, however, the roof was intact.

Trago whistled through his teeth. A man came into the empty doorway.

"Yo," Earl Slade called softly.

Trago rode to the door. "How's things?"

"Just right."

Trago rode to the shed and tied his horse beside the three already there: Slade's, Motley's, and Sullivan's. Carrying a coiled rope, he returned to the cabin. He entered the gloomy, rat-fragrant interior. He could smell Motley's pipe-smoke.

"Where is he?" he asked.

"Here," said Slade, from a corner.

"Let's have a light."

A match was struck, and Will Motley was revealed lighting a candle-stub which he set on a box. There was no furniture in the cabin: neighbors had taken it away to their own homes as soon as the original homesteader gave up. On the floor in a corner, his knees pulled to his chest, sat Dick Sullivan. A mighty puny apology of a man, thought Trago, staring at him. Nothing much to him but some old clothes, thin red skin, and red mustaches. His ankles were tied together, his wrists similarly lashed and brought around in front of his ankles and tied to them. His eyes had a dry, feverish gleam as he peered up at the rancher, who stood above him slapping his leg with the rope.

"They bring the horses?" Sullivan asked anxiously.

Trago slowly shook his head. "We're eighteen head shy."

"Give 'em another twenty-four hours," said Sullivan.

"That'd be too late."

"Too late for what?"

"To set an example," Trago explained. "We've got to bring this to folks' attention so they won't ever forget it."

Sullivan suddenly struggled against his bonds, then relaxed and stared up at the rancher like a trapped fox, full of fear and hate. "You murdering bastards!" he choked.

Trago grinned and turned to gaze out the door. The mauve dusk was drawing like cobwebs across the prairie.

"Long wait ahead," he said. "Better not to leave till after midnight."

Motley walked to the door and looked out. "Where are we going to do it?" he asked. Into his voice had edged the faintest tinge of fear, and Trago's gaze sharpened on him.

"In town," he said. "Why?"

"In town!"

"Where else? We want every man in that camp to see him."

"But—" Motley raised his hands and let them drop.

"You don't have to figure it out. I've already figured it out," said Trago. "Nobody's going to see us."

Motley moved around a bit, glancing now and then at Sullivan, who was frozen in a terrible silence, but breathing like a man with a searing fever. Motley passed close to Trago and touched his arm. They went outside.

"I don't know," Motley muttered, "I'd be inclined to give him another twenty-four hours, myself."

"Why?"

"Main thing we want is the horses. This is going to raise a hell of an uproar."

"You afraid of a little uproar?"

Motley shrugged, and Trago said through his teeth, "I don't know how a man can ranch for fifteen years in the Indian country and come out with the thin skin of a woman. I swear to God!"

"It ain't that, Tom. I'm thinking that it may not end

with us hanging him. It may end with them hanging us."

"The day a cattleman can't stand up to a passel of pasty-faced homesteaders, I hope I'm dead."

It was nearly dark when Farrell regained consciousness. He came awake choking. Old Man Cuff was pouring whisky into his mouth. He doubled over in a spasm of coughing, and each tearing cough was an explosion of pain in his skull. When he had recovered, he sat on the tail-gate of the wagon while the pulsating agony in his head went on blindingly. He touched his head where Trago had slugged him. It was matted with blood. He raised his head and gazed about the camp. There were only three or four men in view.

"What happened, son?" Cuff asked.

"Trago slugged me." He gazed around the shadowy horse-camp. "Did he come back?"

"Not him."

Bill Spence brought a cup of coffee. "'Most everybody's took off. All the boys you hired yesterday are gone."

Cuff put a large bottle of dark liquid into his hand. It had the flask-like shape of a bottle of cough syrup. "Take a big belt of that," the old man said. "It's called Mother Winslow's Soothing Syrup. It'll soothe anything but a broken leg."

Vern drank it. The alcohol burned pleasantly; there was something else in it, too, probably opium, which might burr off the broken margins of his pain. He handed the bottle back.

"What about Sullivan?"

Cuff shook his head. Johnson, a few yards away, was rolling his gear into a blanket-roll. He looked up, a hard-eyed, practical man.

"Do you feel like riding?" Johnson said. "We ought to be on the move. We've just been waiting around for you."

"On the move where?"

"How about Osage? There ought to be a train tonight. East or west—it don't matter much."

Vern let himself down off the wagon, but had to continue leaning against it. "It would matter to Dick Sullivan. If we don't find him, I don't give him a prayer."

"And if we don't, and the boomers find us, I don't give us a prayer."

Vern walked over. He put his foot on Johnson's blanket-roll and gave it a push, so that it rolled out flat on the ground.

"I'm paying you fifty dollars a day. You're still on the payroll." As Johnson reached in his pocket, he shook his head. "And you're not buying out. You can quit—if you're yellow."

Johnson pulled up his belt, staring at him. "Don't ever say that to me when you haven't got a busted skull."

"They're not paying fifty a day for pinochle partners," Farrell retorted. "I'll make you a deal. After we find Sullivan—or know it's too late—you can take off."

Johnson said scornfully, "After we find Sullivan, it'll already be too late."

Vern touched his head again, thought a moment, and finally said, "Saddle me a horse. There's no use staying here. We'll ride up and down the creek. Then if he don't find them, we'd better go on into town."

The candle in the sod-shanty had long since burned out. Sitting on a bench outside the cabin, Tom Trago had dozed a little, in the way of an animal, his whole system of reflexes on hair-trigger. Suddenly he heard a man moving near him. His hand moved slightly and the starlight gleamed like frost on his revolver. It was only Motley coming from the cabin. Motley stared at the gun. Trago put it away. Standing, he stretched.

"'Bout time, I reckon." He pulled out an old railroad watch and held it to catch the cold light of the stars.

"Tom, I don't want none of it," the other man said.

"All right."

Motley blinked, surprised. He rubbed his eyes as though they ached. "I'll go along with him deserving it. But I don't want to be one of the hangin' party. I'm out."

"All right, I said! I figured you'd eat crow. You wouldn't fight when they canceled your Ponca lease, so why would you fight now? Slade inside?"

"He's gagging Sullivan. I don't know how to explain it, Tom, but I never was much for watching a hangin', even a legal one. If a man kills somebody, he should die. But I don't want to see it. And this man didn't even kill anybody. When I was mad, I thought I could go through with it. But now—"

Trago pushed him out of the way and entered the cabin. A few minutes later, he and Slade brought the homesteader outside. "Help us get him on his horse," Trago snapped.

They lifted the man to the saddle. Though it was midnight, it was still oppressively warm. Trago's face was slick with sweat. Motley began explaining again why he could not go along, but the rancher cut in angrily:

"You're afeard. That says all that needs to be said."

"All right, I'm afraid. Afraid I'd have it on my conscience."

"To the point where you'll try to stop us?"

"No. No." Motley shook his head.

Trago gazed at him long and penetratingly, then nodded at Slade, who held the lead-rope of Sullivan's horse. The foreman started the two horses across the yard.

"You stay here," Trago told Motley. "Don't leave this place all night, understand?"

Motley passed both hands down his face, ending with a wiping motion across his mouth. "All right, Tom."

Trago rode after the others. As soon as he caught up, he told Slade: "Keep goin'. I'm going to watch Motley a bit. Wait for me near the county road."

Slade nodded and led the gagged and blindfolded man into the darkness.

Trago waited fifteen minutes beside the path they had come in on. The corn-shocks provided scant cover for him and the horse. He could hear crickets singing everywhere, sawing away even inside the shock of corn which hid him.

Then there was a sudden lessening of their concerted music, and he turned his head to hear what had silenced them. A moment later he saw the horse coming from the sod-house.

Coming along at a fast jog, Motley's hat was pulled low. He looked like a man in a hurry, intent and preoccupied with his troubles. He did not even see Trago as Trago swung his horse alongside the path. Not until Motley's own horse saw Trago and took a single jump sidewise was he aware of him. Motley curbed the horse quickly. Then he saw Trago, who crowded his pony up beside the rancher's. The long-barreled Colt was in Trago's hand. Motley's free hand flew up shoulder-high.

"Wait, Tom!" he exclaimed.

"Lying, sneaking—!" uttered Trago viciously.

"Tom, as God's my—"

It had been Trago's intention to shoot. But when it came time to squeeze the trigger, he found himself reluctant to do so. Friendship—the old days—something prevented him. Instead he let the hammer down and with a sudden motion raised the gun and slashed at Motley's head. Motley ducked, and the muzzle of the revolver raked down his face. The blood spurted. Motley's hat flew off. Trago struck again, solidly this time.

The rancher lost his stirrups; in three pitches the horse threw him to the earth. He lay flat on the ground, as the horse went buck-jumping away into the darkness.

Trago rode off.

CHAPTER 13

With Old Man Cuff, Johnson, and Bill Spence, Farrell rode into town at ten o'clock that evening. They passed completely around the square, looking for Trago's horse at one of the hitch-racks. The tent city was already quieting, the heat having exacted its tribute of human energy. In twenty-four hours the tents would be going down, the wagons rumbling north from town to line up for the run.

They did not find what they were after, and Vern was tense with anxiety.

"We ain't tried the saloons," Cuff suggested. They dismounted at the Cherokee Bar, Spence staying outside with the horses. As they entered, Vern heard Jeff Ridge's voice raised in a loud, emotional declamation. Someone saw the ranchmen and warned Ridge. He stopped speaking, and from the middle of the bar he stepped out to stare at them. There was a long, throbbing silence, as every man tried to read from their faces what had happened.

"We're looking for Tom Trago," Vern said.

Ridge started toward them, moving unsteadily, obviously full of whisky. He was wearing a Colt. Vern watched his hand swing back and forth near the holster.

"You're looking for Trago, are you?" Ridge mocked. "That's funny. We're looking for somebody too."

"You won't find him in a bottle. Why don't you get out and hunt?"

Ridge's red face distorted. "You've already hung him! You murdering swine! You came here to celebrate—"

He tried to draw the gun. While he fumbled at it, men shouted and fell over one another trying to get clear of the fire. Vern ran at him and crashed against him. They went down hard, fighting over the gun. Ridge pulled it, but Vern twisted it from his hand and threw it aside. He hit the boomer on the jaw and Ridge covered up and tried to scuttle away. Vern came to his feet quickly. The room rocked in his vision; he could see nothing clearly.

He had expected to be looking at a gun in someone's hand. But these men, all settlers, seemed to regard him like men at bay. Throughout the smoky room they stood quietly, some with their hands raised.

"All right, son," Old Man Cuff said, behind him. "This is no place for a cowman tonight. It ain't a cowman's saloon any more."

The old man had drawn his gun to cover him. Sturdy and weathered, he stood holding a gun on the crowd. Vern backed toward the door. Ridge was on his feet now, touching his jaw tenderly.

"We haven't got Sullivan," Farrell told him. "Trago's got him. If you want to help Sullivan, find Trago."

Ridge's eyes mocked him. Vern was too tired and ill, depleted by the shock of the sudden conflict, to argue. He kept backing until someone's hand took his arm and guided him out the door. Old Man Cuff came out last, holstering his gun.

Bill Spence brought up the horses. "Sounded like a rumpus in there."

"We can't hang around here," Vern said. "We'll have to wait in camp until we know."

"I think so," Old Man Cuff said.

But when he had mounted, Vern knew he was not equal to the ride back to the creek. He felt giddy and cold. The lights of the tent-town swam with a watery luminescence. The pistol-whipping Trago had administered was still having its effect.

"Go on back," he told the others. "There's someone I want to see. I'll rest a little and be along later."

They tried to argue with him, but he turned his horse into a vacant lot and rode from the main street to an alley which parallelled it. Holding the saddlehorn to steady himself, he passed along behind the buildings. Most of them were dark, but he thought he would know the rear of the newspaper office by its long screened porch. As he rode, it seemed that the saddle was twisting beneath him. He put his weight over to the other side, but the saddle continued to slip, and he seized a handful of the pony's mane to keep from falling. He felt himself going over. The ground met him with a jarring impact. He heard the horse snort and try to back, but he clung to a single rein.

"Who is it?" someone called. It was a woman's voice. He thought numbly, Maybe it's Rachel. Then there was a light around him, and the sound of a screen door creaking. The girl's voice said, "You're hurt! Here—I'll take your horse."

While she tied the horse, he tried to rise. "Don't try to stand up," she told him. "I'll get someone to help—"

"No!" he muttered. "Don't get anyone."

"Well—come inside, at least," she said. She began pulling at his arm to assist him toward the shop. With her help he stood up, but a moment later he became fascinated by a pinwheel of beautifully colored lights. The lights somehow absorbed and chilled him, and they were the last thing he knew.

Trago had seen this town grow up, hating every street and alley of it, but learning its byways as he knew the trails of the Strip. Unobserved in the hot night, he led Slade and Dick Sullivan from the belt of farms around Hogan, through its dark outskirts, to an alley beside Murphy's

Feed Barn, on the square. They had made Sullivan
manageable with whisky. He had drunk a pint before they
reached town, and now, with another half-pint in him,
blindfolded, gagged, and with his hands tied behind him,
he was a loose bundle in the saddle. Slade and Trago wore
handkerchief masks now, blue bandannas pulled up to
their eyes.

Standing in the mouth of the alley, Trago looked over
the street and square. Out there in that parched and
windswept tent-town, a few lanterns still burned. He
could hear babies crying. *Jesus Christ*, he thought, *they
must breed like prairie dogs! How many crops a year?*
Two hundred feet south, Trago made out a line of horses
at the hitch-rail of a saloon, bits of brass and silver in their
harness glinting in the light from the windows.

He moved out onto the walk and scrutinized the front
of the feed-barn.

Above a square door in the loft projected a stout
timber used with a block and tackle when hay was loaded
into the barn. The building was dark, but somewhere
inside a night hostler would be nodding as he waited for
six o'clock and his relief. It was the hostler that bothered
Trago. He studied the problem a moment before turning
back into the alley.

Sullivan was swaying in the saddle and behind him the
rancher could see the masked face of Earl Slade. "How
'bout it?" Slade asked nervously.

"Hold him here," snapped Trago.

He took his rope from the saddle and walked from the
alley onto the walk. He gazed carefully in all directions
before he entered the barn. The building was big, dark
and fragrant, with a mustiness of animals and hay. No
light broke the gloom except for a weak sickroom glow
from an office-lamp. Trago crossed the trampled path
between the rows of stalls. The office door was open. He
moved so that he could look inside it.

The lamp was burning in a wall-bracket, its wick
burned down to a steady rim of blue. Against one wall was
a dusty rolltop desk; in a corner stood a rifle. Every inch

of the walls was covered with calendars featuring lovely ladies, ducks which had come to grief through birdshot and the tender mouths of hunting dogs, as well as lithographs of Indian battles and babies. Scraps of harness dangled from wall-pegs. Trago's eye found the night man asleep in a chair, an old man tilted back with his mouth open and his chin nearly touching his chest. A faint aroma of liniment reached Trago's nostrils.

He drew his Colt and moved quietly into the office. A cat jumped off the desk with a soft thud and scurried out the door. The old man woke up.

Trago moved quickly, his arm making a quick semaphoring movement. Biting deep, the gunbarrel drove the old man back into the chair, which slipped and crashed to the floor. Lying there, he raised his hand and made a fumbling caress over the top of his head, where blood showed in a dark line across his scalp. Trago dropped to one knee by him and waited, but the man slackened out and went back to sleep.

Trago ran from the office. Thrusting the gun into its holster, he seached for the ladder to the hay-loft. He walked to the base of it and looked up. With the rope coiled over his shoulder, he climbed to the loft. The heat was like that of a brick-oven, taking him by the throat and choking him.

He could see the square outline of the hay-door. He stepped around the pyramided bales of hay to reach it, made a noose in one end of the rope and tossed it out over the crossarm. It fell silently and swung crazily for a moment. When it had come to rest, Trago dropped the other end and the simple machinery of the lynching was complete: one rope, one crossarm, one neck.

A hot exultation burned in him. He hurried back to the alley, to find Slade nervously waiting with his Colt thrust against Sullivan's back. "Thought you must of went to sleep!" Slade panted.

"We're all set," said Trago.

Sullivan tried to say something. The gag made it sound as though he were talking under water. Trago rode out

into the street, but just as he was going to signal Slade
forward a man came from the saloon and headed toward
the stable. Trago backed his horse and signaled to the
foreman to hold up. He stayed where he could see the
man, who was obviously drunk.

The pedestrian halted, lurched back, and made a pass
at something, as though slapping at a mosquito. With a
catch of his breath, Trago realized that he had walked into
the rope. He waited rigidly while the drunk swore at it,
looked at the barn, and said, "Why doncha keep your
God-damn' equipment where it belongs?" He weaved on
down the walk and turned the corner.

Trago signaled to Slade. The foreman crowded
Sullivan's horse from the alley and they lined the boomer
up under the crossarm. Suddenly Slade touched Trago's
arm and whispered:

"Tom!"

He was pointing at two men who had just come from
the saloon and were standing on the walk looking toward
them.

They waited. When Sullivan began struggling, Trago
swung a quick blow to his jaw. The boomer sagged, and
Slade had to keep him from slipping to the ground. Up the
walk, the two men who had come from the saloon now
crossed the road and shambled into the big tent jungle.

Trago went to work fast. He dropped the noose over
Sullivan's head. Again Sullivan tried to struggle and yell.
Though his arms were tied behind him, he attempted to
throw himself from the saddle. Taking a couple of dallies
of the rope about his saddlehorn, Trago ordered his
foreman:

"Flog the horse!"

Slade hit the rump of the pony with the end of his reins.
It brought its hind legs up under it and plunged forward.
Trago set his horse for the rope-shock. Sullivan was
yanked like a sack out of the saddle. He swung wildly a
few feet above the ground. Backing his pony, Trago lifted
the man's body higher. Sullivan did not kick; his neck had
been broken by the first jerk of the rope. Down the street,

someone came from a doorway as the running horse clattered past.

Slade threw a quick bight over the hitch-rack, and Trago shook off the dally about his saddlehorn. Sullivan swung six feet above the street in long, uneven arcs.

"Let's get outa here!" Slade panted. "Somebody's chasin' the damned horse!"

Trago feasted himself on a last look at the boomer-camp and the silhouette against the dark sky. Then he turned and followed his foreman back into the alley.

CHAPTER 14

Rachel was unable to lift Farrell onto the cot after she had succeeded in getting him into the small bedroom off the work area. She tucked a pillow under his head and spread a blanket over him. Excitement and concern set her heart to pounding. She built a fire in the airtight stove and heated water for tea.

It was after one when she finished brewing the tea. She decided to go for a doctor if he had not regained consciousness in a half-hour. But when she carried the tea into the bedroom, he was stirring. Resting on one elbow, he gazed dully about. Hearing her skirts rustling, he glanced up and smiled faintly.

"Have I been bothering you again?"

"You had an accident," Rachel said. She helped him to an old Morris chair in a corner beside a reading table. "I'll bring you some tea."

He remembered vaguely riding down the alley looking for something, but he did not remember coming here.

What had happened before that was like a dark pond his mind did not wish to trouble. But a face swam out of it, finally, and it was the sharp-featured, defiant face of the homesteader. When Rachel came back, he asked her:

"What time is it?"

"A little after twelve. Do you feel better?"

"Yes. When did I come here?"

"Over an hour ago. You're looking better, but you have a bad cut on your head. I think you should have a doctor."

He took the cup she handed him and placed it on the flat oaken arm of the chair. "Has Sullivan shown up yet?"

"No. At least I haven't heard about it." Seeing him close his eyes again, she asked anxiously, "Do you really think they'll go through with it?"

"I didn't, until Trago slugged me. Now—I'm afraid of it, Rachel. I'm afraid."

"It would be murder!"

"Not in Trago's eyes. It would be an act of war, and Ridge started the war." He sighed. "I don't know where else to hunt," he said. "There aren't many trees left in the county big enough to hang a man from, but they'd be the place to look."

She clenched her hands in her lap. "I don't know how anyone—any human being—!"

"There's always been a question of whether Trago was human or wolf. You saw him fight the other day. He fights to win—*how* he wins is beside the point. He isn't fighting just Sullivan and Ridge. He's fighting the people who put us out of business. And I think something happened to his mind while he was in prison."

Somewhere beyond the walls of the print-shop, out in the street or among the tents, a man shouted. They looked at each other. When the sound was repeated, Rachel stood up. Her features were white.

"I'd better go see what—" She reached the door and leaned against the jamb, feeling suddenly weak.

Vern rose from the chair. He crossed the room and touched her arm. "Stay here. I'll take a look."

The broken window, through which a homesteader's

stone had crashed the first night, had been patched with
cardboard. Standing in the dark shop, he slid the
cardboard aside and listened. There were several voices
now; a man was running. Out in the tents, a few lanterns
had come on. The running man was coming toward the
shop from the southeast corner of the square. He shouted,
as he passed, "Marshal! Marshal!"

Another voice called, "Get a doctor!"

Still, it could have meant a shooting or a knife-fight.
He stayed by the window. More and more lights were
going on all over the camp. After a few minutes he heard
several men coming back down the walk from the
direction of the marshal's office.

"... I don't see how they could've done it—!" Welty's
voice complained. He sounded thick-witted and dull with
sleep.

"They did! By God, they did! We heard the horse
runnin', and after we caught it we came back and—and
there he was!"

Vern walked back to the bedroom.

She looked at him as he came in, then covered her face
and slumped to the cot. He sat down. "I don't suppose
you'd have any whisky around," he said.

She was weeping. Finally she said, "In Fred's
tool-box."

"If it's all right with you—"

She shook her head. He went out, came back in a
minute or two, and patted a bulge in his jacket pocket. "I
took the bottle. I won't drink here. But I've got to get out
before they start searching for us."

She lifted her skirt to wipe her eyes and nose. "You
can't," she said. "Someone would see you. Besides, you
aren't in any condition to ride."

"If they found me here, they'd probably burn the place
down. That Grant woman hiding one of *them!*"

"You'd have to ride a full day to escape them. And
they'll probably send a posse to watch the trains."

He sat down. He kept thinking about the little bottle of
whisky in his pocket. And he thought of the homesteader

lying on a wagon-bed while a doctor held a mirror to his lips.

"It's so hard to decide who's really to blame," Rachel said faintly. "They'll blame you, and your men, too, even if Trago did it. But it started with Jeff Ridge. And four years ago it was a lot of little fights between homesteaders and ranchers in the Indian country."

"Four years?" Vern said. "Ten. It started with the boomers who sent the homesteaders in under the cavalry's noses, just to create incidents. They built ramshackle cabins, and the army burned them down. Then they went to work on Congress, and lobbied the Indians out of their tribal lands. The boomers had as much right to those lands as the Indians had to Washington, D.C. But the land was good, and they wanted it. And after they got it, they broke it up and found it would raise just about as much wheat and corn as a pile of broken pottery. That's where it started, Rachel. With the Dan Hogans."

She sighed. "The question is, where is it going to end?"

He smiled. "It's mighty tough country, isn't it, for a little girl with a trunkful of temperance tracts?"

"It is," she agreed. "All I know for sure is that you aren't going to leave here tonight. I have one lynching to report in the paper tomorrow—I don't want another. I want you to get on that bed and rest. Tomorrow I'll make a deposition to the marshal that you were here when it happened."

He knew she was right. He would have little chance of getting out of town. And if he did, all he could do would be to start riding. He was not ready to do that. He still had a few horses, if they hadn't been run off. He still had his plans, and now if he had a little good luck to offset the bad, he would be making the run with Spence and Johnson and paying his way to a new start somewhere.

She took his arm and urged him to lie down. Gratefully he lay back. He was too weary to relax. His body and mind were as tight as a bowstring. He watched her bend over the lamp and puff it out. Then there was just a little light from the other room. He closed his eyes, but opened them again when he heard her pulling the Morris chair across the floor. She tugged it through the door into the other room. Then the light went out there, too, and he heard her settling down. Sleep stole over him like a winter fog, wrapping everything in coolness and silence.

Rachel was awakened by the sound of a horse stamping.

Crumpled into a corner of the chair, she opened her eyes and had to think a moment to know where she was and why she was there. A thin gray light seeped into the room through the screened windows. She heard the horse again. She wondered who had come to work so early in the block, and why he had tied his horse in the alley instead of stabling it.

But of course—it was the last day, the day before the Opening. The storekeeper had many things to do this last day. Or it might be a clerk from the land office. No, a clerk wouldn't own a horse, not in this town where a horse brought four hundred dollars if it could walk across the street. This was the way her mind was going, in that vestibule of half-finished sleep, when the truth shot through her mind like pain.

It was Vern Farrell's horse! Standing right there in the alley—a cowboy's horse, a horse which no one could possibly fail to recognize who had ever seen it! A cowboy's horse carrying a roping saddle. . . .

She stood up, shaken, and pushed her hair back from her face. Her shirtwaist was wrinkled and her skirt had twisted half around her. She straightened herself up and hurried to brush her hair. *Now, how,* she wondered desperately, *how can I possibly lead that horse to a stable without its being obvious that I'm hiding him?*

She gazed out at it. It was restless from being tied all night. The poor animal must be dying for water and feed. She saw the coil of rope on the saddle, and realized she could not lead it over that way. Everyone who saw it would know it was a cowhorse.

She stepped out, loosened the rawhide thong which

secured the rope, and carried the coil of rope in and laid it on the floor. She looked at herself in the mirror again. The gray light was stronger. The sleep-lines in her face were still deep. Heavens, she thought, I can't—! But since she had to, she went outside and untied the horse.

The nearest livery stable was Murphy's Feed Barn in the next block. Rachel walked the horse down the alley to the street, turned right at the street and came to the barn. At once she saw a little group of men, their collars turned up in the early-morning coolness, gazing at the barn. She looked up too and saw it then—the short, sturdy timber projecting from the loft of the building. With a sick conviction, she knew it was where Dick Sullivan had been hanged.

Rachel led the horse quickly into the barn. A sleepy hostler was doling grain into troughs in each stall. Seeing her, he ambled to the front. "Yes, ma'am." He gazed at the horse, frowning in perplexity.

"I—I found this horse wandering in the alley behind my home," she said. "Someone will probably be looking for him. I thought he should be tended."

"Well, what do you know!" the stableman said, running his hand over the horse's withers. "That there's a cowhorse!"

"Is it? I didn't see any rope, so I—"

"Look at the saddle-horn—that's a ropin' horn, and it's been used plenty. Where'd you say you found him?"

"Be—behind my home," she faltered.

"Where's that?" He knew she had no home here. He was a townsman and he knew every resident. And he knew she was lying.

"Just up the way," Rachel said. "Will you take care of him? Just hold him until the owner calls."

The stableman gazed at her queerly. "Sure. Sure. I'll hold him."

To throw off anyone who was watching her, she turned down the street instead of up it when she reached the corner. It took her ten minutes to return to the shop. Farrell was awake when she arrived. He looked much better, but he was tense and worried. He had coffee boiling on the stove. He needed a shave badly, but he seemed ready to work now—if there was anything he could possibly do.

"Where's my horse?" he asked her.

"I—I just found him a few minutes ago. I was afraid someone would see it and bring the marshal, so I took it to a stable."

"Which stable?"

"Murphy's Barn."

"Everybody there knows me. Why didn't you wake me up? I'm ready to travel."

"Vern, you can't travel! There are people in the streets already. You couldn't move a block without being seen."

"I'll have to. I can't stay here."

He poured himself some coffee. Rachel said, "I'll make you some breakfast. Whatever you do, you'll do it better with some food in you."

"I don't have time. I'll have to go for the horse before they put a guard on it."

Then they heard the knock at the street door. Farrell set down his coffee. He looked at her. She saw that he had buckled on his gun. His hand touched it.

"Come on out, Farrell!" a man bawled.

He looked at the back door. But now there were sounds in the alley. Rachel saw a man briefly; he quickly ducked out of sight. Farrell took out his gun and looked at it. Then he handed it to her.

"Take this out to Welty, will you? I don't want him getting nervous. Then I'll come out."

Rachel took it. Then she put her arms around him and pressed her cheek against his shoulder, full of sympathy and warmth, and not caring too much if he knew.

"I'm sorry I spoiled things. But you'll be safer in jail. And I'll print the real story and make sure everybody in town reads it!"

Safer in jail, he reflected. Little girl, you've got a lot to learn. . . .

CHAPTER 15

There were three cells in the jail. An old man was sleeping off a drunk in the rear one, Dan Hogan occupied the center cell, and Marshal Welty locked Farrell in the cell over the street. In each cell there was a small, barred window overlooking an alley. After the marshal had finished booking Farrell, breakfast was brought in from a café. Hogan ate with good appetite. He struggled around his cell, moving awkwardly on his splinted leg with a cane to take the weight off it.

A few townsmen began coming to look at the new prisoner. They were awkward about it, standing near the bars to regard him with self-consciously menacing stares. One man muttered, "There's the dirty murderer!"

Dan Hogan looked up from his breakfast. "Which one of us you talkin' about? You've got a choice in this jail, friend."

Welty laughed. He was enjoying his position. "We got the best-stocked jail in the Territory right now."

Welty turned the office over to his deputy, and went out to take statements from the men who had found Sullivan's body.

Tackett, Dan Hogan's lawyer, came to consult with his client.

"I've had some telegrams back and forth with the public prosecutor in Indiana. He knows your reputation, Dan. He may not press for extradition."

"Hell, I'm not afraid of standing trial!" Hogan exploded. "What you're supposed to be doing is getting me out of here before the Opening!"

Tackett deepened his voice professionally. "I've been over every angle of it, Dan. And unless the girl withdraws her charges, there doesn't seem to be any way to get you out. Besides—" he said, uncomfortably, "you don't really think you could ride a horse in your present condition, do you?"

Vern watched Hogan clench his fists. "I'll ride, or drive a sulky—but I'm going in!"

"It's a fifteen-mile ride, Dan," Tackett reminded him.

"I'm going to make it!"

After Tackett left, Marshal Welty returned. He was carrying a coil of black-dot manila rope. He threw his hat on the desk and sat down to write something. Outside, voices could be heard on the street. Welty looked up with a frown.

"Close the door," he told his deputy. He threw down his pencil and carried the coil of rope to the door of Farrell's cell.

"Ever seen this before?"

"I may have."

"Is it yours?"

"No."

"How do you know it isn't?"

"Because I don't use a black-dot rope."

"This is the rope that hung Dick Sullivan," the marshal said doggedly. "For some reason, there was no rope on your saddle when I looked it over this morning."

"It was there last night. I don't know who took it off."

"Where were you last night?"

"I was at my camp for a while. Then I looked around town for Trago and Sullivan. I sent my men back to camp after I had a run-in with Jeff Ridge at the Cherokee Bar. Then I went to the newspaper office."

"Why did you spend the night there?"

"I passed out. Trago'd slugged me early in the evening. I had the trouble with Ridge, and I kind of caved in afterward."

"Who helped you hang Sullivan?"

Vern shook his head. "I told you I didn't. I did everything I could to stop it."

"You held him prisoner at your camp yesterday, didn't you?"

"No."

Welty slapped the rope at the bars. "Damn you, don't lie to me! Ridge swore to me that you captured both of them, and held Sullivan hostage."

"That was Trago's idea. But in the morning, after they'd stolen my horses, Sullivan was gone. I figured Trago'd moved Sullivan."

The door opened. Street noises came in like a gust of wind. It closed, and Vern saw that Rachel Grant had entered. She was carrying the rope from his saddle—he recognized it at once by the rawhide hondo. Welty looked around. He pulled up his lower lip as he frowned at the rope. Then he snorted.

"Just in time! I suppose that's Farrell's catch-rope!"

The girl laid it on his desk. "It's the rope I took off his saddle this morning before I took the horse to the feed-barn."

Welty's wide-spaced teeth were revealed in a rude grin. "Oh, now, miss! This is a little *too* strong! Why didn't you find a rope for him *before* you stabled the hoss, so the story'd hang together?"

"The rope," Rachel insisted, "was in the shop. I'd forgotten it until I came across it just now."

"Why did you take it off in the first place?"

Rachel's eyes met Vern's. Then she looked defiantly at

the marshal again. "Because I knew they'd be hunting every cowboy in town, and I knew he was innocent. I had to move the horse from the shop, but I didn't want it to look like a cow-horse."

"If this cowboy was so innocent, why'd he hide in your shop all night?"

"He was sick. He couldn't go any farther."

"Why did he come there?"

"I—I don't know."

"Farrell?" Welty said.

"I needed a place to hole up for a couple of hours. I thought the newpaper office might be it."

Daniel Hogan rapped on the floor with his cane. "Rachel," he said, with a puckish smile. "Have you got a moment for a wicked old man?"

"What is it, father?"

She gazed at him soberly, but Vern saw a smile try to touch her lips. Hogan hobbled to the door of the cell. "Does this young man's welfare mean much to you?"

"Yes. Of course. I know he's innocent."

"Pretty sure he's innocent?"

"Certainly! He was with me from midnight on—"

"Why couldn't he have taken part in the lynching before he came?"

"Because there were still too many people around before midnight. He—he would have been seen."

Welty interrupted doggedly. "I know for a fact that him and Trago and the rest of the cow-crowd made their brag that they'd lynch Sullivan. That's admissible evidence, Dan."

"Maybe so. But I'll bet Tackett could have him out of here in two hours for lack of evidence! If I told him to, that is."

"Fine. There's a parcel of boomers out in the street who'd give him just as quick service."

"Not if I called them off."

Welty's face darkened. "Dan, you're meddling where you've got no—"

"I'm talking to my daughter. How about it, Rachel? Can you forget you brought those warrants from Indiana? For just two days? Long enough for me to put those people of mine on the good claims before the sooners and tinhorns grab them all? That's all I ask."

Rachel bit her lip and turned away. She gazed across the room. Welty's big hand gripped a bar of the cell.

"Work out any deal you want, Dan, but don't drag Farrell into it! He's guilty as Cain—you know it. If you'd seen Sullivan hanging there last night—! His neck stretched out like taffy, his tongue swole out of his mouth, and his face as black as—"

Rachel turned away quickly. "Marshal, we don't need a picture! Father, no. I can't."

"Why can't you?" Hogan demanded wrathfully. "Are you still all snarled up in right and wrong and whisky-drinking and votes for women?"

Rachel's chin raised. "In the first place, I don't trust you. I know how many promises you made my mother. But how many did you keep? For all I know, you wouldn't make any effort to free Mr. Farrell. As a matter of fact, you have him right where you want him, haven't you?"

Hogan looked at Vern. "I've got nothing against him. When I thought he'd brought you here to use against me, I could have killed him. But apparently I was wrong."

A wagon was moving along the street, going over the potholes with a hollow clatter. It stopped before the jail, and the sounds of men running and calling questions came through the barred windows. After a few moments there was silence. Vern heard a familiar voice.

"That's right—take a good look! And don't ever forget it."

Footsteps came up the walk. The door opened and Jeff Ridge was standing there looking over the office. He had put on a dark suit, his black hair was tousled, and there was a lacquer of excitement on his ruddy, battered face. He came in, nodded to the marshal, and gave Hogan a brief, businesslike smile. Ridge was playing a big part. He came now to the boomer's cell and peered in at him.

"How are you, Dan?"

"For an old man, pretty fair, Jeff. What's all the excitement out there?"

Ridge looked at Vern. "They're wondering how long they're going to have to wait."

A frown crossed Hogan's face. "Wait for what?"

"For justice! They've seen Sully. Now they want to see somebody else get it."

Hogan's leathery face toughened. "They'll damn' well wait until somebody's been tried before they see anybody 'get it'!"

Ridge looked surprised, but he adjusted quickly to the change in weather conditions. "That's what I told them. But most of them are pretty restless." He put his hands in his pockets and moved before Vern's cell to gaze at him gloatingly.

"Well, we've got one of them, anyway!"

Rachel snapped: "This man had nothing to do with it. He was with me all night."

Turning his head, Ridge smiled at her. "Oh, he was! All night, eh? How about that, marshal? Guess that ain't too unusual, eh—a man spending the night with a woman after a lynching?"

Vern wet his lips and glanced at Rachel. "Why don't you come a little closer to the bars, Ridge?" he said.

Hogan said, "Shut your mouth, Jeff! You knew what the lady meant."

"Dan, all I said—"

"I heard what you said! And I know what you meant, and I want to hear you apologize to my daughter for it."

Ridge was stunned and silent.

"Did you hear me?"

"But, Dan—She may be your daughter, but she's the one who put us all in a bind! And now she's trying to protect one of the men who lynched Sully!"

"You heard me!"

Ridge rubbed his neck, shrugged, and told Rachel: "Sorry I said it—ma'am."

Rachel smiled winningly. "Oh, that's all right! I

imagine you say such things to all the girls, Mr. Ridge."

She turned to Vern. "I'll do what I can for you. I'll print the truth, at least."

"Think about that proposition, Rachel!" Hogan called after her as she went to the door.

With her hand on the knob, she deliberated. She opened the door, but stopped in the opening to gaze into the street. "No! *No!*" she whispered. She backed from the door and turned a white face toward the cells.

"What's the matter?" Welty asked. He walked to the door and looked out. Vern saw him thrust his head forward curiously. "That's Dick Sullivan, ain't it?" he said.

Ridge uneasily massaged the knuckles of one hand. "Thought it might be a good idea for folks to see him before he was put away. So I borrowed a wagon and—"

Hogan stumbled to the bars. Staring at Ridge, he whispered, "You miserable—idiotic—!"

"Dan, I thought it was the least—"

"It *was* the least. It was the least sensible thing any man could do—to put his friend's body on exhibit! Another lynching—is that what you're after? Drag your filthy swamp-rat's carcass out of this town and don't ever let me see you again!"

"Dan, that ain't fair!" Jeff Ridge argued. "I've done a lot for you—"

"For me? For the free land you thought you'd get out of it. Get that wagon out of sight before people think I had anything to do with it!"

Ridge looked at him, his hurt beginning to melt away under the heat of a growing anger. He gazed around at the watching faces with their contemptuous eyes, and a determination came out of its sheath bright and keen. Without a word, he turned and walked to the door. He closed it behind him and went down the steps to the street. People were clustered thickly about the wagon to look at Dick Sullivan. Someone reached in to brush the black September flies from his face. As Ridge climbed to the seat of the wagon, they grew silent, seeming to wait for a

statement of some kind from him. He waited until it was
quiet. Then he said in a low voice:

"It looks like Farrell will get off."

"Get off!" a man exclaimed.

Jeff Ridge nodded slowly. "That's right: get off. That's
the way it looks right now."

CHAPTER 16

The heat packed in on the jail, dry and dust-laden. Through the morning and early afternoon they heard the noise of moving wagons and teams, men's voices shouting in the square and the clop of horses. All movement was north. Wagons and riders were heading for the line to jockey for positions. Lying on his cot, Dan Hogan stirred painfully.

"The sound of a dying city," he groaned. "A city dying and a dozen others being born. And I'm out of it."

Something clanged against the bars of Vern's window. A rock clattered on the floor. Hogan looked at it and then spoke angrily to Welty:

"Marshal, how long are you going to let those fools hang around out there?"

Welty, shirt-sleeved and unshaven, hunched over his desk. "I can't stop them unless they try to come inside. There's no law against peaceable assembly."

"When they get through assembling, they won't be so

peaceable. But it may be too late by then to do anything about it."

Welty gave a sly grin. "You're forgetting something, Dan. This is the last night before the Run. Pretty soon they'll all be moving up to the line and they won't have time for Farrell. I'm waiting them out."

Hogan snorted. "They haven't all got horses to make the Run, and the ones that haven't are the trash you've got to worry about."

Welty gave him a fatuous smile. He leaned back and linked his hands behind his head. "Why don't you let me do it, then, and quit fretting me? Farrell," he said, "you ain't sayin' much. Ain't you worried?"

Vern squinted at him. "I was just sitting here wondering how I'd handle it if I were you."

"Reached any conclusions?"

"I think I'd turn me loose as soon as it's dark. You've got the girl's statement that I was with her when it happened, so there's really no evidence. I'd unlock the back door and tell me to take off."

Welty frowned, chewed on it, and sauntered down the brief hall to the rear. He came back. "You wouldn't get far, cowboy. There's two men on the roof of a shed across the alley."

"Let me worry about that. In the dark I wouldn't make much of a target."

Welty sucked a tooth and frowned at the street door. "It ain't dark yet," he said thoughtfully.

Trago and Slade spent most of the day in a thicket beside a dry creek. They could hear wagons moving on the county road. Flies and gnats deviled them and the horses. The horses switched their tails, and Trago, reclining on the ground, smoked wheatstraw cigarettes and kept an aura of bitter-gray smoke before his face. There was a smell of warm earth and sage. He dozed a little that afternoon, and now, as the shadows stretched, he ate some jerked meat. His foreman was inspecting a fore-hoof of his horse.

"Figuring to travel?" Trago asked him.

"Soon's it's dark."

"What's the matter—gettin' spooky?"

Slade let the horse lower its hoof and stepped back. "This ain't cow-country any more, Tom. Sunbonnets, hayseeds, and plows! It makes me sick. I'm for Texas."

"You haven't got two nickels in your jeans. You going to leave thataway?"

"Been broke before," Slade said. He frowned and scraped under his thumb-nail with the blade of his knife.

They had not discussed the lynching after the flight from town. Trago was not sure how his foreman was feeling, but he seemed to smell fear and disgust on him. Slade had been half full of whisky when they strung up the boomer, and maybe all the bravery had sweated out of him now.

"Texas," said Trago reflectively. "Man with a little stake might do right well in the Big Bend country."

"Man without a stake could punch cows." Slade shrugged. "You buy a spread and I'll punch cows."

"I've got no money either," Trago said. "I sold my beef for next to nothing when I lost my leases, and I haven't made a dime since. But I bet I know where there's going to be a lot of money. . . ."

Slade narrowed one eye and paused questioningly in his nail-cleaning.

"In the Strip," said the rancher.

"Those dirt-poor farmers? A thousand dollars would buy out a dozen of them."

"It wouldn't buy out a couple of banks." Trago smiled. He held his cigarette caged in his hand, letting the smoke leak out through his fingers. "Remember last time? There was banks before there were decent saloons. One feller had a wagon he called a bank! It's going to be that way again."

"You going to borrow money from a bank?" Slade asked.

"Borrow it the way they borrowed our land. They get it back when they catch us."

Slade snapped the knife closed. He shook his head, his long face stern. "They'd catch us, too, Tom. They've been catching a lot of them night-riders lately. And they'd catch us."

"The ones they've been catching didn't know when to quit. That's why they got caught. I'd quit when I had my stake. A week, two weeks, and we'd be ready to break up the bunch and drift."

Slade dropped the knife in his chaps pocket. He chewed his lip. He was a tough and realistic man, but this seemed to stop him. "Just the two of us?"

"If need be. I count on one or two others coming along."

"After last night? Huh-uh."

Trago rose and brushed the earth from his jeans. There were sparks like steel in his eyes. "After last night they'll know there aren't enough farmers in Oklahoma to stop us! By God, Slade, that was just the start!"

Slade rubbed his jaw. "How can you put it to them now? You like to killed old Motley, didn't you?"

"Motley's an old woman. I don't need his kind. But Old Cuff's mucho hombre. If I handle him right, he'll come along. There's you, me, Cuff—maybe Farrell. . . ."

"You even got him lined up, eh? Last night you split his skull. Tonight he answers roll-call in your army."

Trago squinted. "I know that boy, Slade. I laid the rod to him more'n once when he was a young'un. And that'd always bring him around. By now he'll know I was right. At least I'm going to find out. Saddle your horse," he said.

Slade, looking dubious, saddled his pony. They jogged south toward the horse-camp.

Since last night, Old Man Cuff, Bill Spence, and Cole Johnson had been waiting at the horse-camp. Motley had come in, bloody and sick, and told of being pistol-whipped by Trago. He had had enough: before noon he rolled his blankets and rode out.

They were all nervous and undecided about what to do next, for they knew what had happened to Vern Farrell, and while they were anxious to ride out of here, they felt an obligation to stick by him. But no one had come up with a good idea for releasing him from jail.

A man set his foot on a twig. They started, turning to stare at the brush. Tom Trago stepped from behind a tree, a rifle in his hands, a ragged cigarette dangling from his lip. A muddy burgundy sky of sunset was behind him. Looking at Old Man Cuff, he began to chuckle.

"How'd you ever last so long in Injun country, old man?"

Cuff opened and closed his fists. "I'm out of practice, Trago. You're practically the only Injun that's left. You bloody wolf!"

Keeping them under the muzzle of his rifle, Trago sauntered in. "I had the guts for a dirty job, that's all." He turned his head and whistled. In a moment the sound of horses came through the trees. Trago looked around the clearing. "Where's Farrell?" he asked curiously.

"Where's Farrell?" Cole Johnson echoed sourly. "Where the hell do you think?"

Trago narrowed one eye and studied the camp, as if he expected to find Farrell hidden somewhere, holding a gun on him. "Well, where is he?"

"In jail!" Johnson said. "Where else?"

Slade came riding in, leading Trago's horse.

"In jail!" Trago stared at them.

"At least he was in jail when Johnson went in town this morning," Cuff said. "He could sneak in because he ain't dressed like a cowhand, like the rest of us. Maybe they've taken Vern out and hung him, by now."

"In jail!" said Trago. He looked stunned.

"You were talking about bunch-quitters the other day," Cuff accused. "Ain't seen a worse one than you. Put a pardner in jail and leave him to be lynched!"

"In jail!" Trago muttered again. "How'd he land there?"

"We went looking for you. Vern took sick from the lick you gave him on the head. We had to leave him in town, and they arrested him in the morning."

"You left him in town!" Trago blurted. "What the hell did you think would happen?"

"He wasn't in shape to ride," Cuff said defensively. "He said he had a place to stay. It seemed like the only thing to do."

Trago kicked savagely at the ground and walked closer to them. "What're you going to do about getting him out?"

"What *can* we do?" Johnson retorted. "Three of us against the town! Maybe you've got an idea."

"A mob of plow-pushers lynch a cowman!" said Trago incredulously. He squatted to light his cigarette at the campfire. Slade had dismounted and left the horses standing ground-tied. After a moment Cuff began speaking.

"I'd as soon tackle the town as not, if there was a chance of getting him out. But what chance would we have?"

Trago rose slowly, puffing on the cigarette. "What chance? That's the whole trouble with this outfit. You gamble like farmers—a dime-limit game. I wanted to make a fight a long time ago."

"You can't fight a prairie-fire with a tin cup," Cuff replied.

"You can if it's full of dynamite," Trago snapped.

They were silent. Trago burned the cigarette up in a few long puffs. He threw the butt into the fire.

"If you had any guts, we could have him out of there in ten minutes," he said.

"It'll take more'n guts," Cuff retorted. "Take my word for it. It'll take a big idea. You got a big idea?"

Trago gazed into the fire, the lines of his face easing. "I've got an idea. Have you got the guts?"

"For anything that makes sense."

They were all listening to him now. He stood with the firelight enhancing the harsh pockets of shadow in his face. "What about a game that would put money in our pockets and shake Farrell loose, all at once? Does that make sense?"

"Might."

"All right. Hear me now," Trago said curtly. "Slade's taking cards in this game. With one or two more, we can't miss...."

He told them what he had told Slade, speaking with his eyes glinting and his hands clenched hard on the rifle. He made them see the quiet streets and the sudden, shocking invasions of the cracker-box banks, the horsemen leaving as boldly as they had come; then the long night rides to the next town, in an unexpected direction and in an unpredictable manner. He mentioned the probable take for each of them, and even old Cuff's eyes took a golden gleam. But at the end, their minds took a farther reach than his, and they saw the gallows and the line of nooses waiting for them....

Cuff shook his head. "I'm too old to hit that trail. Don't know about those fellows...."

Trago looked at them. Spence shook his head; then Johnson. Trago's mouth twisted. "Gutless damned chicken-farmers! You couldn't pry yourselves out of a gopher-trap!"

"You keep talking about guts," Johnson pointed out, "but I don't see you doing anything but talk."

Trago gazed at him. "What time is it?" he said.

Cuff pulled a watch from his pocket. "Quarter to eight."

"All right. I'll have him out before nine o'clock."

"Big talk!" Johnson scoffed. "You haven't seen the mob."

"... And I'll make him the same proposition I've made you. And I'll bet he goes with me and Slade. He's seen 'em clear, now—their mouths open yellin' for his neck! He knows what I've been talkin' about."

"Tell you what ain't clear," said the old man: "How you're going to get him out. Do you want us along, or don't you?"

Trago picked up the reins and toed into the stirrup. He stared down at them scornfully. "I wouldn't ride across the road with you. I'll get him out and put him on a horse. And when you hear about it, you'll know I did it alone."

CHAPTER 17

Just before sundown, Rachel returned to the jail with Tackett, the lawyer. She was carrying a copy of the *Oklahoma Warrior*. The crowd in the street had grown, and Tackett had to bull a way through for them. A wagon was parked at the edge of the street, and Jeff Ridge and several other men were standing on it. Ridge had been haranguing the crowd.

When they reached the steps, Tackett went up and hammered on the door. "Marshal Welty!" he shouted.

The door was opened six inches and a rifle-barrel came through. As the opening widened, Welty was disclosed standing just inside. Beside him, armed with a shotgun, stood his deputy, Carl. As Rachel started up the steps behind Tackett, a man seized her arm.

"What's your hurry, miss? Lots of men here just as good as that lonesome cowboy. Give you all the lovin' you need—"

The lanky attorney suddenly turned and drove his fist

into the man's face. He pushed Rachel into the jail ahead of him. The mob shouted, and Tackett dived inside after her. Welty slammed and locked the door. Something struck the door and clattered down the steps.

Farrell had come up off his cot when he heard Tackett's voice outside. He was emotionally exhausted; his mouth was as dry as plaster, and the muscles of his neck were rigid. At first he had thought, *They'll get tired of it and drift away*. But they hadn't. They had been promised a show, and they were not accepting excuses.

Farrell watched Tackett take a paper from his coat pocket and hand it to the marshal. "Miss Grant's agreed to the release of Dan Hogan," he said.

Welty shook his head. "No can. He's awaiting extradition to Indiana."

"Read the paper," Tackett suggested.

Opening it, the marshal read a few words, but shrugged. "What is it?"

"A *habeas corpus*, signed by Judge Fawcett. Miss Grant believes she's made a mistake—that Dan Hogan is not Daniel Grant."

"That what this says?" Welty walked to his desk, laid the paper down, planted his hands beside it and propped himself over the paper to read some more of it. "Okay," he said. "I guess that's good enough."

Hogan lumbered up and went to the door. "What about Farrell, Myron?"

Tackett produced a second paper. "Another of the same, marshal," he smiled. "Lack of evidence. No complaining witnesses."

"Fine!" Welty told Vern. "You just walk right out, cowboy. The town's yours."

Hogan turned to Vern. "Stay here till I come for you. I'll take Ridge down a couple of notches and beat that mob to its knees."

Tackett gloomily watched Hogan limp from the cell. Shaking his head, he said, "I don't know how a man with his ankle in splints can lead an army to victory."

"I'll get a sulky somewhere," Hogan said. He sounded a little desperate.

"That'll look good—you jumping gullies and creeks in a sulky! Dan, you'll be all day getting to Pawnee townsite. And without you to guide them in, those boomers of yours will be running around the prairie blind as moles after a plowin'."

Rachel looked at Vern. "No doubt Mr. Farrell would be glad to lead them."

Hogan glanced curiously at Vern, who frowned and gazed out the window into the alley. It was dark now, but the presence of waiting men could be felt there. "I had a little game of my own planned," he said. "A few town-lots."

"Why couldn't you still take the lots?" Hogan began to warm up. "You can't use more than a few, anyway. You're the only man besides myself who knows one square mile of the area."

Outside, Vern could hear the sound of wagons and horses, and the voices which had been shouting his name all afternoon. "Is helping them a condition of my getting out?" he asked.

"Of course not."

"Then it's no deal. They're out there yelling for my neck. I've got no obligation to any of them."

"Those aren't my people," Hogan protested. "The men I'm talking about—"

"They're all your people. The Territory's full of your people. You brought them, didn't you? You beat the big drum that brought them on the run."

Hogan looked at him a long while, reflecting. At last he said, "You'll think differently when you're out of here. I don't blame you. Marshal, unlock the door. And let's have a lamp so they'll know who's talking to them."

Welty unlocked the door. He and Carl stood aside as Hogan and the lawyer moved out. There was a roar from the crowd. Welty closed the door and wiped his mouth with his sleeve.

They could hear Dan Hogan shout: "Listen to me—!"

"Been listening to you too long, old man!" shouted someone.

"Then you can listen for two minutes more...."

The mob listened.

Inside the jail they listened, too. He was a good orator; a countryfied Dan Webster, and he made his voice and his choice of words work for him. He used his voice like a trumpet; he berated and exhorted them, working up to the moment when he would say, *"Now, why don't we all get back to work?"* At last he said it.

A moment later there was a crash of glass. Someone swore. Someone yelled. Then the crowd began to shout. A stone hit the door. Welty opened the door quickly and the two men fell back into the room. There was blood on Tackett's hand, where the broken lamp had cut him. Welty slammed and locked the door.

"As God's my witness," Hogan raged, white-faced, "I'll kill Ridge!"

Hogan raged, Tackett listened thoughtfully, and Welty paced the floor. "Got to do something pretty quick, by Joe!" he announced.

Vern saw that Rachel was weeping. "I was going to do such big things!" she whispered. "Close the saloons—turn the *Warrior* into a force for good—and I couldn't even stop one man from getting drunk—a man who wanted to stop. And I couldn't make that crowd believe the truth."

"You're too ambitious, girl," Vern said. "Those are two of the toughest tricks in the deck—reforming drunkards and selling the truth."

Hogan had made up his mind. "I'll round up some men of my own and tackle that bunch another way. Welty, unlock the back door. Rachel, you'd better come back to the shop with me."

"I'm going to stay here," she said.

Hogan looked at her. He appeared about to insist; but then he saw something in her face that changed his mind. "All right," he said. "Maybe a woman's still the best force for good in the world. Must be about the last in Oklahoma, though, way things look."

Welty produced a lantern and saw the men out the rear door into the alley. There was no trouble from the men in back, and Welty returned to the office alone. He frowned at the clock on the wall.

"Five to nine," he muttered.

"Make a note of that, Carl," Vern said wryly.

CHAPTER 18

Trago and Slade had ridden up from the south, jogging along a few rods off the main road. Before leaving the horse-camp, they had saddled one of Farrell's ponies to bring along. Scores of rigs and horses were on the road, making for the imaginary line two miles north of town behind which the cavalry would hold them until noon on the following day.

Near town, Trago halted. The trail dipped through a shallow draw where there was heavy brush and a few cottonwood trees. Trago looked over the scene carefully. A hundred yards away a wagon rattled past on the main road.

"This'll do," he told Slade. "We can't lead his horse in—might be spotted. I'll ride in and get him out. My horse can carry double this far. Then we'll be in the Strip in a half-hour."

Slade's brow creased. "Tom, how in tophet do you think you're going to get him out of that jail?"

Trago pointed at the glow of the nearby town. "Know your weather-signs, cowboy? Watch the sky!"

"I don't get it."

"You don't hafta."

"Pretty sure Farrell will take cards in this game of yours?"

"If I wasn't, I wouldn't be bothering with him."

Slade glanced about uneasily. "When will you be back? Some boomer might decide to cut up this draw."

"I'll be back in a half-hour."

Trago skirted the town, working around to the northeast corner of the settlement. He wanted to come in as directly as possible. He stopped on the edge of the main road north, where he could see and hear the huge traffic of horses, men, and vehicles moving up to the Line. He gaped at the dark pageant flowing by.

My Lord, what an exodus! he thought—like something out of the Bible! People riding, walking, driving every kind of vehicle he had ever seen. Children bawling in covered wagons, dogs barking, wheels grinding and creaking like a column of artillery.

Trago rode on into town. In the crowds, he was merely one more horseman hurrying along. He halted at the nearly deserted hitchrack of a general store on the south side of the square. From here he could put a long, sweeping gaze on the square. He watched the traffic working out in all directions from the tent city, like ants from a scorched hill. Most of the tents had already gone down. But in the center of the area remained a little community of tents and covered wagons.

Gazing across the square, he saw that the street before the jail was blocked by a crowd. There was a wagon parked in front of the jail, and a lantern gleamed on the seat of it, looking orange through the dust. He could hear men yelling, and now and then something would strike the door of the jail.

Trago grinned. The hounds baying after the treed 'coon! Well, now, let's have something to bay about, he thought.

Head up, he rode boldly into the square. A west wind blew steadily into his face. He could feel the grit in his teeth. Pushing through the glut of settlers was like swimming upstream. As he made for the still-intact core of the camp, Trago watched the fires. Fire and blood: there had always seemed to be a kinship between them. Both were hot, the heat of a fire scarcely less scalding than the jet that shot from the skull of a cow-critter when you dehorned it; or the bright stream pouring from the veins of a throat-slashed hog. Fire was life, and blood was life, and both were so close to the heart of things that you had your finger right on the pulse of it when you dealt with either one.

Everyone seemed to be loading a wagon or hitching a team. Somewhere they were singing a hymn. Elsewhere a concertina wheezed, and farther away men were laughing. Trago was in the middle of the camp, now, threading the canvas alleys, looking for the right place.

There was a canvas shelter stretched between two wagons as a windbreak. The wind kept it bellied and taut. Trago felt a pulse quiver in his throat and he knew this was the spot. Halting the horse, he put a cigar in his mouth and pulled some matches from his pocket. He lighted the cigar. Then he made a little bundle of the matches, glanced around and saw the alley was clear for a moment. He put the tip of the cigar to the match-heads. They fizzed up angrily. Trago thrust them against the canvas. Almost instantly it caught. It blackened, reddened, burst aflame, and a hole as big as a silver dollar showed in the canvas.

Almost instantly a woman screamed *"Frank! The tarp's on fire!"*

Fire!

Everyone was bawling it at once. Trago rode on. Never looking back, he heard them running to extinguish it, heard the clatter of galvanized buckets and the frightened shouts. A tent attracted his eye. Pulling out some more matches, he set fire to them with the cigar and held it to the canvas. Then he rode on....

When he left the camp, they were already fighting four separate fires.

Unhurriedly, he paced along, listening to the uproar. The fire-bell before the engine-house was bonging out its bronze hysteria. The volunteer hose-men—if they hadn't already left town—would be dragging the hose-cart and engine into the square.

From the next corner, he gazed up Kickapoo Street. The wagon still had the street half blocked before the jail, but the crowd was gone. Trago rode on, not pushing, just taking his time and letting things develop. In a few minutes he came into the alley which passed behind the jail and gazed up it thoughtfully.

Not a soul in sight. Trago came to the jail. He could taste the smoke and hear the yelling in the square. Behind the jail was a shed with a stout iron hasp in the door. He laced the reins of his horse through the hasp and dismounted. Then he rubbed out the cigar against the brick wall of the jail and dropped it and, walking with a soft chime of spurs, he moved up the side-alley to the street.

In the square there was a hell of an uproar, and Trago's teeth showed and his dark mustaches looked like those of a pirate. Settlers were scampering about like ants. The pumper was going; the volunteers bowed frantically to one another across the engine as they see-sawed the brakes up and down. A puny jet of water was being used to soak tents which had not already caught fire. Each tent, as it caught, flamed briefly like a moth in a lamp-chimney.

A man ran past the alley-mouth and darted up the steps and into the jail. Vaguely, Trago remembered the high-shouldered look of him. Myron Tackett—Hogan's lawyer, he recalled. Trago drew his Colt and walked into the jail after him.

Farrell saw Trago before the lawyer did.

Tackett was unlocking his cell with Welty's keys, talking as he did so. Welty had gone out to help fight the fire, but Rachel was watching the fire through the window.

"This is your chance!" Tackett panted. "We'll go down to the shop and bring you a horse later. You can ride to Osage and catch a train there."

Tackett threw the door open and turned to stride back through the door. He stopped short on seeing the rancher. Vern looked at the gun in Trago's hand. Tackett began raising his arms.

"No—!" he said.

"Get in the cell," Trago said, and to Rachel: "You too, lady."

Vern stared at him in astonishment.

Trago took Rachel by the arm and led her to the cell. Tackett had already obediently backed into it. Trago motioned Vern out. Vern stood aside, not sure what was going on, but very sure that Trago was dangerous. Having locked the cell door, the rancher pulled out drawers in the marshal's desk until he found Vern's gunbelt. He drew the gun, set the hammer at loading position, and spun the cylinder. The gun had already been unloaded. He thrust the Colt back into the holster and tossed belt and gun to Vern, who caught it. Vern never took his eyes off him. He could not understand why Trago had come back.

"Let's go," Trago said.

"Where? What's the idea?"

"What do you care where, just so it's someplace else? Come on!"

Trago was still holding the gun on him, and it was no time to argue. He shrugged and walked to the door. He looked out, and though there were men running down the street, no one was looking at the jail. It struck him that there might be more than coincidence in Trago's appearing just as the fire broke out.

He looked back and waved his hand to the girl and Tackett. "At least they won't hang this one on me," he said.

"Let's go!" Trago said again.

They stepped out. The fire was already ebbing, since there was little to burn that was more substantial than paper. It had flared up, and now it was settling, a few wagons burning, an overcast of smoke drifting with the wind across the town. Vern left the jail and Trago kept pace with him.

"Down the alley," Trago said. "Got a horse in back."

They ran down the alley to the shed in the rear. A horse was tied here, Trago's big apaloosa. Trago mounted and freed his left stirrup so that Vern could use it to swing up behind him. "Have to ride double a spell. I got you a horse outside of town."

Trago rode south down the alley, worked through side-streets to the county road, and followed it a short distance before cutting east to a minor road which ended before long in the fields. Looking back, once, Vern discerned a reddish radiance in the sky.

In the hot and moonless night, they rode across sun-scorched fields and plowed strips until they came to a dry wash. Trago rode up the wash a short distance. Then he halted and gave a whistle. Someone whistled back.

"That's ol' Slade," Trago said, sounding proud.

Slade was waiting with two horses. Vern slid off Trago's horse. He suddenly felt good—strong, free, alive. He flexed his arms at full length and crossed them, then looked at Trago and waited to be told what came next.

"Told 'em I'd bust you out!" Trago grinned. "Don't recollect you saying thanks."

"Don't recollect lynching that settler they were going to hang me for," Vern retorted.

"Me lynch him?" said Trago innocently. "No, sir, I turned him loose. I reckon he must've had enemies."

Vern did not argue. There was a crazy, wild shine on the man. He felt somehow that he had crossed a line, that killing would come easily to him now, that he was not one to argue with.

"What about my bunch?" he said. "Have they taken off?"

"No. They're waitin' for you. That waitin' didn't get you out of jail, you notice."

"What about that fire?" Vern asked. "Is that what got me out?"

"Fire?" Trago said, looking blankly at his foreman. "I didn't see any fire, did you?"

"Not from here," said Slade.

"There wasn't no fire," Trago said.

Farrell shrugged. "All right, where do we go from here?"

"North."

"How come? North's trouble. Everybody's heading north."

"But everybody ain't going as far as we are. We're going into the Strip."

"Tonight? The line's patrolled. They'd spot us and we'd probably land in a stockade as sooners."

Trago laid a hand on his shoulder. "Now, you know a little passel of troopers can't see everything that goes on. Come on! Let's ride."

CHAPTER 19

The line was an almost tangible thing, as definite as a wooden barrier. Hundreds of settlers were in temporary camp behind it. Some had been there for days. Others were still moving up, coming up against it and spreading out east and west to take up their positions. Fires glowed in a long line passing over a hill a mile or so to the west. They were lost in brush and rough ground to the east.

From the knoll where they had pulled up, Trago pointed at something due north of them. "There's a cavalry camp yonder. Main camp's fifteen-miles west. There's about thirty troopers working out of this one, and another bunch three miles east. There's a cannon on that knoll, there, that they'll use to set the farmers off tomorrow."

And yet with all this evidence of a movement so big the President himself probably could not have stopped it, Trago could not see that the sun which had set a few hours ago had set forever on the old days. Vern felt the strength of an emotion coming up to them on the breeze, caught in the smoke of a hundred fires—the emotion that would keep every man and woman in Oklahoma and Kansas awake tonight. The stir of big things, the fear of being left out; and yet the conviction that it couldn't happen to them. They had come too far, staked too much on it, to lose now.

Vern estimated that the riders coming from the north and south would meet in the middle of the Strip about a half-hour after the Run started. Those would be the fast and lucky ones. The site of Pawnee, the metropolis-to-be, was a few miles this side of the center-line, so that there was an advantage in making the run from Oklahoma. And that was why there were more boomers milling around down here tonight, selling each other maps and readying their stakes and flags, horses and wagons.

"Best chance of getting into the Strip's a couple of miles east," Trago muttered. "It's brushy there, and nobody's going to try to make the run through the brush."

"Why do you want to go into the Strip? If you're figuring to hide out, there's going to be ten thousand homesteaders wandering around there tomorrow."

"Why don't you just keep your mouth shut for a while?" said Trago.

They rode east on a line paralleling the boundary of the Strip, until the land began to break up in gullies and dry creeks, with dense brush covering it. Here and there a campfire could be seen, an ember of red in the night. Once they heard a small cavalry patrol going by with jingling harness. Trago turned north up a dry wash with low cut-banks. They rode for fifteen minutes.

Suddenly Vern heard a sound above the soft scuff of their horses' hoofs.

"Tom!" he said.

Trago's head turned questioningly. Vern pulled up. "Listen!"

Over the breathing of their ponies could be heard the plodding of horses behind them.

Trago drew his rifle from the boot. Slade pulled his

revolver. Vern eased his Colt from the holster and began loading it; it was not lost on Trago, who snapped:

"Don't get clever with that Colt! Load it and put it away."

"If it's cavalry, what are you going to do?"

"Whatever I have to."

"Aren't you in deep enough already?"

Trago did not reply. The hoof-sounds were closer; there was no question that the riders were coming toward them. Goose-flesh ran up Vern's arms. For some reason it seemed to be his lot to be saddled with Trago's recklessness. It was foolish to come into the Strip; it was suicide to go to war with the cavalry. He thought, with a sudden yearning which squeezed his heart, of Rachel that night in the print-shop, the soft gold of the lamp on her face, and the velvet of her lips when he kissed her. It recalled a peacefulness he might never know again.

The horses were close now, and a man's voice said a few words in a gruff undertone. Something in the sounds pulled at his attention. He whispered suddenly:

"It's not cavalry. We'd hear their bridle-chains...."

Trago frowned, then looked pleased. "Usin' your head."

He rode boldly to the center of the wash, making as much noise as he could with his horse, letting it dance around while he spurred and reined it at once to keep it stirred up. Down the wash the other sounds pinched off in sudden, shocked silence. *Sooners,* Vern thought—men sneaking into the Strip ahead of the other hundred thousand homesteaders. Trago held the horse finally, trembling between spur and bit.

"Halt!" he shouted. "Who goes there?"

There was no sound from down-wash.

Trago bawled again: "After them, men! Don't let a mother's son escape!"

He spurred his horse down the wash but pulled up sharply. There was an explosion of startled voices and a thunder of horses running. Vern grinned. The sooners were in full flight before the fancied cavalry patrol.

Trago came back, and they rode on a quarter-mile before they halted again. Distantly they heard some shooting. Then the prairie was silent again. Either the sooners had run into a real patrol, or had fired some shots to slow down their pursuers.

"This ought to be far enough," Trago said.

"Far enough for what?" They had dismounted and Trago was lighting a cigar.

"For a pow-wow. Ain't you gonna ask why I came for you?"

"I figured you'd tell me when you were ready."

"I'm ready." Trago blew cigar smoke between them. He squatted on the sand and made marks with a branch. "We're in trouble. Reckon you know that."

"I'd about figured it out."

"Then we might as well make it worth their while to catch us, eh?"

"You, maybe. Not me. After the excitement dies down, there'll be a coroner's inquest over Sullivan. I've got proof that I was somewhere else when he was hung."

Earl Slade chuckled. "Don't you know who'll set on that coroner's jury? Farmers. Twelve farmers will set there and decide whether you're guilty or not. Man don't need second sight to know how it'll go."

It might be true; but the foreman forgot something. "When I turn myself in," Farrell told him, "it won't be in Hogan. I'll pick another town, and ask for a change of venue. Besides—Hogan will testify for me."

"Hogan!" Trago grunted. "Man, you've been keeping bad company. That comes of laying around jails. I don't care who testifies for you—they'll stretch your neck if they ever catch you in Oklahoma again."

Vern shrugged, not sure yet what was in Trago's mind, and not wanting to irritate him too far until he knew. He knew the tough and stubborn grain of him, and would not willingly go against it when Trago was in command.

Watching Vern closely, the rancher leaned back and gazed at the brush above banks of the wash. His dark features brooded. "Remember how this country used to be? Before they broke it's back and crippled it for good?"

"Sure, I do. I remember branding calves a couple of miles up this wash, once."

He remembered when the nearest neighbors were Ponca Indians, fifteen miles away. When you rode for months without seeing anyone but your Indian landlords and cowboys; when you trailed your beef-cattle to the railroad in Kansas and stayed around a few days until the town you had thought you would never get enough of began to shrink upon you like a cheap shirt. He remembered how it was to be self-sufficient, master of your own destiny.

But he knew all that was finished. And he had been able to accept the passing of it.

"You remember how they killed your uncle?" Trago prodded.

"I haven't forgotten."

"Sometimes I think you have. He was shot in the back by a homesteader."

"They tell me the homesteader was shot a few days later."

"No," Trago said. "He was dragged to death behind a horse. I laid for him at the spring he'd fenced in."

"Then it evens up, doesn't it?"

"The big thing ain't evened up. It don't even up that they ran us out of business and we never got a nickel for it."

"We never will, Tom. We had a go at it, and we missed."

"The big chance is just coming up," Trago said with a smile. He drew hard on the cigar. The night was hot, with mosquitoes singing in the brush. He blew the smoke between them. "The Dalton boys," he said. "The Jameses.... Butch Cassidy's Hole-in-the-Wall Gang. Make your blood run faster?"

"Those are dead men you're talking about," Farrell said, understanding now what was in Trago's mind.

"Cassidy ain't dead. He made the game work for him, and when he was through he quit—cold. They say he's in South America."

"Some of the boys who rode with him are cold, too."

Trago suddenly gripped his wrist, his face intense. "Listen to me! Here's the chance we'll never have again! Here's fifteen or twenty little towns springing up from the prairie—and money in all of them! Here's banks with walls like crackers—or operating in tents. No sheriffs or marshals—no law anywhere in the Strip! But nobody touches the money. It's like it was a game, and the rules say you can't touch it. Well, damn it, what if we make our own rules? What keeps us from riding off with half the money in the Strip! By God, we'll be square with all of them!"

Trago's energy and tension drove him to his feet. His fist clenched, the cigar in his teeth, he waited for Vern to answer. Slade was leaning against his horse a few feet away. His rifle was still in the boot. Trago's hand was not far from his Colt, but he was not thinking about it. I might get the drop on them, Vern thought. But he knew one or the other would reach his gun.

Then they heard the shout up the wash. It was a cavalryman, calling a hard, peremptory command. Afterward it was silent. The insects and small animals in the brush grew quiet.

Trago seized the reins of his horse. "God, we've got to get out of here! Well, what about it?"

"Tom, we've got nothing to square with those boomers," Vern said gravely. "They came here for land. And they've got a right to it."

"A right! What about us? What about the Indians?"

"The Indians got a raw deal. It was their country—they owned it. But we were just tenants."

"We gave them the only cash they had! We helped them breed up their herds. . . ."

"I know. It was a good thing for them. But now it's done. We can't help that. All we can do is tell ourselves that more people will benefit by cutting up the Strip than will suffer."

Trago took a step toward him, his mouth pulling sourly. He seemed to have forgotten the horsemen up the wash.

"Don't give me any of your mealy-mouthed prattle! Is that what they told you in Washington? Well, I'm telling you it don't matter who you give stolen goods to—they belong to the man you stole them from!"

"I know," Vern said, aware that Slade had moved from his horse and was standing ready for a cue from Trago. "But those people we passed on the road matter too, Tom. I guess I had to see them all in one place, with their patched britches and scrawny kids, to know that. This country's growing. You can't bottle all the people up in the cities without having an explosion sooner or later. You've got to let the pressure off somehow."

Breathing hard, Trago confronted him. "Okay. Let 'em have it. But let's have ours too, huh?"

Vern rubbed his neck. "I came close enough to a hangrope tonight. I'm staying clear of it from now on."

Closer now, a horse struck a rock with an iron shoe. Trago glanced that way. He looked back. The whole meaning of him seemed to become compressed into a bearing and an expression. He was silent, cocked like a gun, wrathful, menacing.

"I didn't ask pay for bringin' you up," he said. "When your uncle died, I split the herd with you down the middle. I taught you your trade. This is the first thing I've ever asked of you."

"I know that. But it's the last thing I could give."

Trago regarded him steadily, stepped back and swung onto his horse. "Then you'd better take off. Me and Slade can handle it alone."

He looked at his foreman. Some meaning seemed to pass between them. Vern glanced sharply at Slade, whose dark, thin-lipped face betrayed nothing. But Slade stood there while they waited for him to turn to his horse. In

order to mount, he would have to turn his back to them,
unless he swung the horse and put it between them.
Keeping his gaze on them, he moved the horse around.

"That's no way," Trago jeered. "Makes a man think
you don't trust him."

"That's the way you taught me." Farrell turned the
stirrup to his boot and started to swing up. Then he saw
Slade drop to one knee, drawing his Colt as he did so.
Vern dropped back, pulling his gun, and went to his knees
behind the horse. Slade, expecting him to swing into the
saddle, fired across the horse. The flash illuminated the
wash. The gunshot pulsed like a massive drumbeat
against the ears. The horse tried to run, but Vern clung to
the reins. His heart convulsed, then raced. Then there was
a flash of anger in his head, and he cocked the gun and
aimed it at the vague shape of the foreman, and fired.

The gunflashes left him blind. He heard Slade make a
queer, moaning sound, and fall. Then he heard a horse
moving—a loud scramble of hoofs, a little slide of
rocks—and he knew that Trago had put his horse up the
bank. He stayed low behind the horse. His vision clearing,
he saw Tom Trago on the bank, just at the edge of the
wash. Trago was searching for him, a revolver in his hand.
But suddenly there were sounds from a hundred feet up
the wash—horses running and a voice shouting something. Trago fired three hit-or-miss shots into the wash
and sand particles peppered Farrell's hands and face.

As Trago reined away into the brush, Vern fired. Yet at
the last moment something caused him to deflect his
aim—an unwillingness to put a bullet into this man who
had been a godfather to him. But as the gun kicked, Trago
changed direction. His horse crossed Vern's line of fire,
and Vern knew he had hit him—that feeling of a hit
flowed solidly up his arm. Trago's horse carried him into
the brush.

The horsemen were sweeping around the last turn.
Farrell weighed it—whether to let himself be taken and
tell his story, or make a run for it. He sprang into the
saddle and spurred the horse down the wash.

CHAPTER 20

In two minutes of hard riding he had gained sufficient lead to leave the wash. He sent the horse lunging up the bank and into the brush. As he rode through the thicket, he listened for sounds of pursuit. After a few minutes he reined in. He could hear only the labored breathing of the tired horse. Then the warm night brought the sound of a shot. Afterward there was a far-off crashing of brush.

He rode farther, working southeast. Again he halted to listen. Still he heard the crashing of brush, but now it was more distant.

He let the horse pick its own trail, until suddenly the brush ended and he was at the edge of a plowed field where a withered crop of grain rattled in the wind. Then he knew that he was out of the Strip.

He looked for landmarks. In the distance a small fire burned against the blackness, ruddy and cheerful—a party of homesteaders, waiting out the hours. He felt like a soldier who, stealing into enemy territory, glimpses a sentry's watch-fire and is impelled to give it wide berth. Yet there was no reason to fear the homesteaders any longer. It was not individuals who had tried to lynch him: it was a creature called a mob. That creature had died in the fire. And now the whole population of Hogan was oozing away down the small roads and trails from town.

He took bearings and rode toward the camp on Comanche Creek. He thought about Slade, lying in the wash with a bullet in his body. From the way he had fallen, he was sure he had been mortally hit. He had never killed a man before, and there was a strange feeling in knowing that he had closed forever a door which had been opened forty years ago.

There was no further pursuit, and a feeling of freedom and excitement began to come over him. It was hard to believe that anyone was still waiting for him at the horse-camp. But if Bill Spence and Cole Johnson and a couple of horses were still around, why not use them? It had all blown up, the original plan, but perhaps he could salvage a little for himself.

Crossing the last field, he smelled woodsmoke and then a wonderful aroma of coffee. Through the giant pecan trees, he could see the fire. He crossed the creek and rode toward the camp. Horses were moving in the field, dragging their hobbles. He rode into the clearing where the fire burned.

No one was in sight.

The wagon had not been moved; a couple of saddles were dumped beneath it. He dismounted and gazed about, then walked to the fire and lifted the coffee pot; it was full. It had not gone dry with resting on the coals. He had a strong sense of being watched, and he straightened and searched the camp with a slow, careful gaze.

"Hey!" he called.

A spur tinkled. Someone walked into the clearing. He turned quickly. Old Man Cuff came toward the firelight. Then from other points appeared Bill Spence and Cole Johnson. They looked at him, and the old man chuckled.

"B'God, I give him credit. He said he'd get you out. He did get you out, didn't he?"

"Trago?" Vern looked at them, glad to be with his own kind again, to see Cuff's ancient face and Spence's knobby jaws and Johnson's calm, dark features. "He got me in and he got me out. Did you see the fire?"

"We thought the damn' town was afire!" Spence said. "What happened?"

Vern told them.

"I don't know for sure whether he set the fire," he said. "I didn't stick around to see whether anybody was hurt. But it looked pretty bad."

He unsaddled the tired horse and rubbed it down with a gunny-sack. He went back and got some sardines and hard-tack out of a box of provisions. He washed the food down with three cups of coffee, and sat wearily with his back against a tree, gazing at the fire.

"Think we ought to put that fire out?" Spence suggested nervously. "Them boomers might take a notion to come out here."

"Not tonight. They're on the move—the whole town. They might not even connect the fire with my being gone."

Johnson looked at him cynically. "We've got two days to go on that contract. What do you want us to do to earn our money?"

"No change," Vern said. "We're making the Run."

"Just like that?"

"Who's going to notice us? I'm not wanted for anything. How many horses have we got?"

"Twelve," Cuff said. "Thirteen, counting yours."

"All our riders have taken off, eh?"

"All but these fellers. Even Motley quit."

"You going to make the Run?" Vern asked him.

Cuff drew on his warped brown cigarette. "Come this far. Might as well see it out. I've got no money to leave on anyway. The poor get poorer, and the rich get richer," he sighed.

"Suppose we sell the extra broncs for cash? We can't

make the Run without riders, and it's too late to find any."

"Where'll we sell them?"

"Up at the line. There ought to be a little cash floating around."

"Then what?"

"Then we make the Run. You'll get one claim, I'll get one and a share of these fellows'!"

Cuff pulled out a silver watch with great deliberation, opened the case, and studied it. "We better be ridin', then. Get up to the line, and rest the horses after we get there."

Vern stood up, feeling every tired joint move. His back was lame from riding and a kind of deadening weariness thrummed in his body. When he thought of saddling and riding again, he wanted to sink down and close his eyes. But they would not be opening the Strip twice because somebody was tired. And it was time to leave.

"Okay," he said. "Take a little food, or you won't eat tomorrow."

They saddled, rounded up the extra horses, and started north.

They had to get off the road for the last two miles. It was congested with vehicles of every kind, and a thousand horses. When they arrived at the line, dawn was breaking clear and with a promise of heat.

Coming over a knoll to look down on the crowds, Vern was reminded of Easter Sunday—everyone up early and out at the camp grounds to sing and watch the sun come up. Along the line itself was a column of men, horses, wagons, and buggies of every kind. Stretching endlessly east and west, they waited for the cannon that would thunder a few hours from now and start the greatest race in history. Behind the line were tents, clusters of settlers, and a few troopers riding about.

It was too late, now, to find riders for the extra horses, for there was no chance of getting registration papers before starting time. They agreed that the best deal was to sell the extra horses for cash. Cuff took four horses and Vern kept five, and they left them at the foot of the hill in the care of Spence and Johnson, and went looking for buyers.

After an hour Vern had sold two horses for cash. The buyers were obviously speculators, not farmers. They would try for a profit on the horses; that failing, they would try for claims, which they would sell. Nearly every man Vern talked to wanted a horse, but not many had cash. That was the trouble with the whole hangdog army of them, he realized: practically no one had two dimes to rub together. How had they ever gotten this far?

He was asking five hundred dollars at first, and then cut it to four hundred. A young farmer gave him two hundred on account and went off to try to raise the balance; but he came back empty-handed.

"I sure wish—I wish I could give you a note for the rest," he said nervously. "If I get a claim, I can borrow on it."

He bit his lip and furrowed his brow then, and Vern knew what he was thinking. *Is it better to start farming in debt, and know you probably won't be able to pay it off, or not start at all?* And while he waited for Vern to decide, a young woman, obviously his wife, waited anxiously on the seat of their wagon, a weathered wagon with a sorry-looking farm-horse between the traces.

"Oh, hell, take it for two," Vern said suddenly.

The man stared at him. "You mean—full price?"

"That's what I mean."

The homesteader had already seen the horse, but he grew dubious. "He's sound, ain't he?" he asked.

"There's nothing wrong with the horse. The trouble's with me. I'm not a horse-trader." He looked at the gold coins in his hand. "Does this leave you any cash?"

"No, but it'll put me on some land, at least."

"What are you going to eat this winter? You haven't even got time to make a kitchen crop."

"Well, I—I figured I'd put in my winter wheat, and then get odd jobs in town."

"That's what they all figure," Vern said, and he could feel the money slipping through his fingers. "There won't be work for everybody, friend. You'd better take this back—"

To his own surprise, he gave him a hundred dollars.

"Well, shoot!" the settler blurted, looking at the coins in his hand. "Well, say, I wouldn't feel right—"

"I wouldn't either," Vern told him. "Better pick up your horse and start gettin' him used to you. I hope you can ride bareback, because there's no saddle included."

"I've got a surcingle, I was hoping to pick up some kind of a saddle animal. Say, I—I sure . . ."

His gratitude somehow nettled Vern. "You may not thank me after this winter," he said. "Even if you get a claim, you may not make a crop. And if you make a crop, there may not be anybody with cash to buy it."

"You can't discourage me now." The homesteader grinned. "This puts the blessing on the whole thing, as far as my wife and I are concerned. The name's Osborn—you remember it and look us up sometime."

Oh, hell, Vern thought, how could you talk any sense into them? They were bound and determined to go to hell in a bucket, and why try to explain to them what you had seen the last time? Nevertheless he hadn't the heart to charge what he could get for the horses, and he made the price a hundred and fifty after that.

Another horse went when a breathless homesteader found him in the crowd and said that a man named Osborn had told him he was selling horses at a right price. Did he have any left? Vern took him over to the horses and gave him his pick of the last two.

Then he put a lead-rope on the remaining horse and rode out into the county-fair throng to sell it. When he heard a buggy rasping alongside him, he glanced around. A big, white-haired man was driving it with one leg propped awkwardly on the dashboard. A young woman was driving with him. They both looked closely at Vern, making sure they recognized him, and then Dan Hogan grinned and Rachel gave a smile of pure relief. Hogan extended his hand. Vern reached down to grip it.

"We weren't sure whether we'd be seeing you today,"

Hogan said. "We heard a man was killed in the Strip last night. No one knew his name. We've done some worrying."

Vern opened his mouth to tell them who it was; but he hesitated. He was sure he could trust them, but he was not sure he wanted to trust anyone with that story.

There was a pause, while they seemed to wait for him to go on. "Well, aren't you going to tell us what happened after you left town?" Rachel asked him.

"Trago had a horse waiting for me just out of town. He tried to sell me on a crazy scheme of plundering banks after the Run. He was sore when I wouldn't buy stock in it."

"Did he start that fire to get you out of jail?" Hogan asked.

"I don't know. I have a feeling he did."

"I know seven people who won't be making the Run because of that fire," Hogan said, his face hard. "They weren't killed, but they were badly burned. I don't know how many settlers lost their possessions—everything they had."

Hogan looked at the horse Vern was leading. "I hear you've got some horses to sell. Anything suitable for a man with a game leg?"

Vern smiled at Rachel. "I'll bet I can find something suitable. How about a rocking chair? Are you going to make the Run in that contraption?"

Hogan shook his head. "My daughter will watch the fun from this. "I've got a sulky over yonder."

Vern saw the two-wheeled cart at the edge of a little crowd of settlers. A sleek black carriage-horse was in the traces, and a man was holding it by the headstall.

"Do you know Brandy Creek?" Vern asked Hogan.

"Are you joking? I know every wrinkle in the land between here and Pawnee."

"That'll be the first wrinkle you'll come to—and it'll be the last. Why don't you save yourself another broken ankle and stay home?"

"Because damn it—excuse me, Rachel—I can't! I've

got promises to keep. And I'll be blasted if I'll let all those good town-lots go to the kind of trash I see on the fast horses this morning—the same kind of tinhorns who grabbed all the good claims last time."

Tackett left the group near the sulky and came to the buggy. "Dan, will you come over here a minute? We've got a problem...."

Hogan started laboriously to dismount from the buggy, but Rachel stopped him. "Why don't you drive over? I'll wait here."

Vern handed her down, and Tackett got into the buggy and drove off with Dan Hogan. Rachel looked around, seeming to enjoy the excitement. The crowd at the line was deepening. Troopers rode up and down before them, crowding back the ones who crossed the plowed furrow in the earth.

"Did you bring your tracts along?" Vern asked the girl. "I've seen a lot of souls around that could do with saving."

"Don't joke about it," Rachel told him. "It's a very serious thing. So serious that I—I've given up the temperance work."

He was surprised. "Why?"

"Because I wasn't sure about my motive in doing it. I seemed to be more interested in taking something *bad* away from people than in caring whether they had something *good.*"

"Such as?"

"Well, in this case, land. A chance to make a living. That's what my father has been working toward for ten years. It's kept him from drinking, too, so it must be better for him than my tracts were for Bill Spence."

"It hasn't been very good for me, so far," Vern told her.

"But can you look at all these homesteaders without feeling that something *had* to be done for them? And besides—you've got a better chance to take a claim than anyone else in this whole crowd!"

Farrell squinted. "For some reason I can't seem to see myself as a farmer."

"Neither can I. I see you always as a man on a

horse—not walking behind one. Did you tell me where you are going when you leave Oklahoma?"

He grinned. *"If* I leave, I might bid on some government forest leases in New Mexico or Arizona."

Rachel's eyes glowed. "Forest leases! It sounds wonderful. I've always loved the mountains—"

"You'll always be a greenhorn, Miss Rachel." Vern smiled. "Those mountains are tough on cows. They hide in the woods, and a roundup that should take a week takes three. And sometimes they work off more beef hiking up and down cliffs than they put on."

"Still, it compares favorably with the life most of these people will have, doesn't it? So why won't you help them?" she asked suddenly.

He looked at her, and let a smile come. "Whatever you're selling, you sell it all the time, don't you?"

"But there's nothing to hold against them now, is there? You know you can't have the Strip yourself, and you don't envy what they're getting. So why not help a few of them?"

"Guide them in, you mean?"

"That's all." She looked up at him, her face appealing.

He gazed at the throng along the line. The sun was higher and it was growing hot and dusty. The cavalrymen were having their time keeping the homesteaders from straining across the boundary line. Several men who were going to make the Run on foot were parading around in distance-runners outfits which resembled knee-length underwear. Map-sellers were still moving through the crowd. He saw Hogan's buggy returning. It stopped and Hogan glanced at Rachel with an expression he was unable to mask completely: *Did you talk him into it?* The whole thing, then, had been a plan to let her work on him alone.

"Did you solve the problem?" Rachel asked him.

"Nothing serious. We're trying to work out a plan to find work for the people who don't get claims."

Rachel took Vern's arm. "Mr. Farrell is considering taking your place today!" she said brightly.

Hogan looked at Vern for confirmation. "I'd say that was an overstatement," Vern said. "If I could help without hurting my own chances—"

"How could it hurt your chances?"

"Well, in the first place a mob like yours couldn't keep up. I can take in my own men about as fast as I can ride. But if I try to help twenty or thirty of them, we'll all drag along with the slowest man, and probably get lost."

"There are only twenty-five of them," Hogan stated, "and they're all well-mounted. The understanding all along has been that a man who falls back is on his own. We'd play by your rules," he declared. "You set the pace, and they keep up or lose out. They'd understand that."

"That might be the understanding, but you know how it would work out. I'd be bushwhacked later by the ones I left behind!"

Hogan glared at him for several moments, and finally snapped: "I'm not going to get down on my knees and beg, if that's what you're waiting for."

"Father," Rachel protested, "you can't blame him if—"

"I do, though," Hogan cut in. "I blame any man who can look at a crowd like this and not be moved by it."

"I was looking at it through bars, last night."

"If you're going to hold Jeff Ridge's actions against every man in the Territory—then God help you! Get in," he told Rachel. "We've got things to do."

"All I'm saying is that every man here is out for himself," Vern said. "I've got to look out for myself, too. Isn't that what you're doing?"

Hogan picked up the reins. "It's on your conscience, not mine," he retorted.

They drove off. Vern was left with an unexpected stab of loneliness, as he saw the buggy with Rachel's hand gripping the side-rail disappear into the crowd.

CHAPTER 21

Eleven o'clock.

The temperature was over a hundred degrees, and a south wind was burning every blade of green. On the knoll behind the line, the cannon which would be fired at high noon was being tended by a half-dozen artillerymen. Miles away in both directions were posts where other cannons were being readied. As far as the eye could see, a throng, sheared off clean in front like a file of soldiers, but uneven and ragged in back, trailed down the boundary of the Cherokee Strip.

Every man in sight carried a little flag on a stake. He carried his registration certificate in his pocket and his hopes in his eyes. And every man was the enemy of the man next to him. Before night, there would be fights and perhaps killings over disputed claims. They gazed out through the shimmer of heat over a flat land with a few trees, and tried to see the monuments and markers. There was nothing to see, unless you knew the country.

Farther out, the range crumpled into low hills, through which would stream-beds, most of them dry. Still farther was a flat land, rich and dark, where the grass stood tall and only a man who had ridden the country for years could tell you where the markers were. A few good all-year streams sparkled under the trees. And out there in an elbow of the Pawnee River lay a big checkerboard of staked claims which represented the town of Pawnee. A small detachment of soldiers had been camped there for a week, keeping out the sooners.

Pawnee was almost due north of the Hogan starting point. You could take off in a straight line, wear your mount out crossing gullies and breaking through coverts of brush, possibly finish the horse off in quicksand, and be at the town-site in something under an hour. Or you could ride northeast, make the easier gully-crossings, take the trails through the brush, and be there in twenty-five minutes.

Eleven-fifteen.

Old Man Cuff said, "Ought to be looking for our jumping-off place, don't you reckon?"

"No hurry," Vern said. "Let them have their spills— we'll stay out of the pile-ups. Fifteen seconds after that gun goes off, it'll be plain where the fastest riding will be."

"Now, as I get it," Cole Johnson said, "we find a lot nobody's already on, and pound the stake on it. That it?"

"That's it. Then you write the time you took the claim on the flag, and take the number from the marker. Enter that on the flag too. Then we come back and record the lot-number and registration certificate at a land office."

"That's simple enough," Spence said. "All we got to be is there first."

"That's all," said Cuff drily.

Eleven-thirty

The line was almost solidly packed with homesteaders. A horseman suddenly broke from the front rank and rode

across the ground, flogging his horse with his claim-stake.
Two cavalrymen immediately spurred their horses after
him. He raced on until a shot was fired over his head.
After this, he meekly allowed himself to be captured. The
troopers dismounted him, took his horse, and escorted
him back to the line afoot.

Farrell looked for the black, fringed buggy in the
crowd. He was almost sure he saw it some distance behind
the line. It was impossible to find the sulky in the throng.

"Man, this is one hell of a passel of people!" Old Man
Cuff muttered.

"Too many for this child," said Bill Spence. "You say
you're going to New Mexico after you sell your land?" he
asked Farrell.

"That's the general idea."

"Well—if you need a sober, reliable ranch-hand . . ."

Vern frowned at his watch, then looked for the black
buggy again. Funny thing about women. How important
they got to seem; even at a moment like this when history
was being written, a man could find his eyes and his mind
wandering toward them.

Eleven-forty

A small group of settlers made a false start when a
pistol was fired somewhere. They stopped immediately as
a half-dozen cavalrymen swept upon them from one of
the guardposts. But their places had been absorbed by
other settlers, and there was a squabble when they
returned.

Farrel squinted through the hot, dusty air. He was
sure, now, that it was the Hogan buggy. In twenty minutes
the cannon would roar, and any chance of anything's ever
working out between him and the girl would be over.

Cole Johnson was checking his saddle-cinch, setting it
up a little tighter for the race. Bill Spence put a finger
under his latigo and gave it a tug. Old Man Cuff was
nursing a crooked cigarette. There was an increasing
noise from the crowd, an incessant, murmuring babble of

hundreds of voices. On the knoll, the officer in charge of
the cannon consulted his watch. A trooper rode up to
consult with him.

In the Hogan buggy, a handkerchief was waved.
Farrell straightened, his heart picking up. Had she waved
it at him, or was she merely fanning herself? Or was it just
the heat making it look that way?

"Well, I reckon—" Cuff began.

Vern suddenly turned to his horse. "I've got to see a
man. Wait here."

"You've got to see a man!" Cuff echoed, outraged.
"That gun's going off in fifteen minutes! What's the
matter with you?"

"I'm not sure. But I'll know pretty quick. If I'm not
back, you boys can take off on your own. But I'll be
back."

"Well, I'll be damned!" Cuff said, watching him
mount.

He rode down the line until he came to the buggy he
had been watching. It was Hogan's, all right. Rachel was
sitting in it, fanning herself with a folded newspaper.
Sensing that someone was beside her, she glanced around.
She smiled doubtfully at him, and then said:

"Isn't it time you got ready for the race?"

"I'm ready. Did you wave at me a minute ago?" he
asked intently.

"No. I didn't even know where you were."

"I thought you waved."

"And you rode over to find out? You might lose your
place, Vern."

"That's all right. You're sure you didn't wave?"

She laughed. "Does it matter?"

He considered it. "No, but it seemed like a good excuse
for me to look you up."

"Why did you want to?" she asked. There was
something gentle about her now, and he thought what a
sad thing it would have been not to have come, and to
have missed seeing it.

"I wanted to tell you a cowman can change just as easily as a temperance girl. If your father still wants a guide, I'll take those sad-eyed boomers of his along. But they'll have to keep up."

She smiled and reached for his hand. "I was so sure you'd change your mind that I've hardly been depressed, even."

"What made you so sure?"

"Everything about you. I just knew."

"Since you know everything else, maybe you can tell me where your father is."

She pointed with the fan. "In there somewhere. He's up on the line, and Mr. Tackett and the others are all with him. If you're going to help them, you'd better hurry." She turned the little chatelaine watch on her bosom.

Farrell started toward the line, but swung back. "Hang onto that horse when the cannon goes off. You might get to Pawnee before we get there ourselves!"

He pushed through the crowd. Other horsemen stared resentfully at him as he went through. Some of them called angrily at him, and finally a man seized his arm.

"Not so fast, brother! The end of the line's back yonder."

"Where's Dan Hogan?"

The settler squinted at him. "Are you with him? I don't recollect you."

"I'm new, and I've got to find him. There's a change in plans."

"My God!" the man said. "Have they put off the opening?"

"Not that I've heard. Where is he?"

"Straight ahead. Dan!" he called. "Dan Hogan! A man to see you."

From somewhere in the clot of riders ahead, Hogan's voice rose. "Who is it?"

Vern pressed on until he could see the sulky. "Farrell!" he called.

Hogan twisted on the seat of the sulky. When he saw

Vern, his face seemed to clear itself of a dark tension. His eyes gleamed, bright and hard. "What's the problem, cowboy?"

"I've got room for a couple of passengers. Any of your people want to come along?"

Gazing at him steadily, Hogan said, "If this is a trick—"

"It is—and it's on me. Your damned hungry-eyed homesteaders have been the ruin of a good cattleman. We've still got ten minutes, if they want to go with me."

Hogan was regarding him suspiciously. "What caused this sudden change of heart?"

"It's not so sudden as you might think. It's my mind I changed."

Hogan grinned and reached his hand up. Vern hesitated a moment, and then took it. "What do you want us to do?" Hogan said simply.

"I want your riders to stay right where they are when the gun goes off. There's going to be wagons and horses piled all over the place when this mob breaks loose. We'll wait just long enough to spot an opening, and then take off."

Hogan debated it. "I guess that makes sense. Which way are you going in?"

Farrell told him. As he finished, Hogan nodded. "You know your trails, all right. Now, some of these people will be going for homesteads. Point out the main markers to them as you go in. But most of them are after town-lots. We've got merchants, a blacksmith, hotel-keepers, a couple of lawyers—everything a town needs. We've got everything but what the town we're leaving has nothing else but—trash."

He spoke to the men nearest the sulky. "You know the rule. Pass it around: keep up or drop out."

Vern told him quickly: "I'm pick up my men and be back. We've got ten minutes."

He worked free of the crowd and rode back to where his men were waiting. Johnson was looking at his watch, sweating and nervous. "Five minutes!" he said. "Are we making the Run, or aren't we?"

Vern told them what he had worked out with Dan Hogan. Cuff looked at him incredulously.

"And Hogan fell for it?"

"For what?"

"For letting you lead them into a blind alley and ditching them, I s'pose. What else would you do for them?"

"I don't know how to explain it, Cuff, but I feel like we might as well leave with good feelings as with bad. It won't cost anything to take them along. Trago figured the other way, and it hasn't done much for him. . . ."

He had scarcely thought of Trago since last night. But Trago was out there somewhere, wounded, and full of the acid of hatred, and perhaps making plans for a coup. He was the war-chief who could not adapt himself to times of peace; the sharp-shinned hawk; the knife that went rusty in the sheath. But he was alone now, and hurt. Being alone had never been a deterrent to his rapacity, however; but if he were sick with the shot he had taken, the hawk might be earth-tied at last.

"Let's go," he said. "We're moving over to Hogan's spot."

They rode over and got in position behind the settlers, signaling to them that all was ready. A kind of humming quiet had come over the area now. Nearly every man had a watch in his hand, and every man's eye was on the artillery detachment on the knoll, watching the officer standing with his saber in one hand and a watch in the other. Vern was conscious of the long, slow, thudding pulse-beats of his heart, of a tingling excitement. He kept his eye on his watch.

Twelve-o'clock—straight up!

It was going to happen now. It had to happen. It did. But when it happened, it was in a way that caught everyone by surprise.

CHAPTER 22

A gunshot popped in the hot air. Farrell's horse quivered, but he held it, knowing it was a false alarm. Then a man shouted:

"That's it!"

A horse broke from the line into the open. For a moment the racing horse was alone, flailing up a cloud of dust as it ran. Then other men were shouting, other horses broke into the clear; and all in an instant a huge section of the line crumbled forward, a broken dam, an avalanche of horses and wagons thundering across the ground. The dust sifted up so that their outlines were blurred and indistinct. A wagon went over and the horses drawing it fell in a tangle of harness. The cavalrymen, clustered before the line to maintain order, saw the horde coming and turned prudently to ride with them.

Vern hesitated. Up and down the line, within a span of two miles, could be seen peaks and valleys in the line where other sections had given way. He could see Hogan's

171

riders turning to stare quizzically at him. He turned his
gaze up the hill at the cannon.

At that moment it recoiled visibly, a plume of pale
flame spurting from its muzzle. Gray-white smoke rolled
forward, to be torn away by the wind. The bellow of the
shot pulsed against the abdomen.

He turned his head. The body of the line, so solid a
moment before, was shredding apart. Individual riders
spurred forward, wagons clattered through openings, and
a few foot-runners lunged over the hot ground carrying
stakes and flags like relay-racers' batons. A runner fell; a
rider swerved to miss him and crashed into another horse;
both went down. A buggy-horse reared as it reached the
tangle, and a rider following too closely behind the buggy
crashed into it. His mount went to its knees and the rider
went over the horse's head.

Threshed from the ground, the dust drifted high.
Farrell waited until the wind thinned it sufficiently that he
could see the tangles and the openings. Then he waved at
Old Man Cuff and the others. He took off, passing
through Hogan's crowd at a jog.

"Here we go!"

The prairie was already dotted with racing horses two
hundred yards out. Ahead and to the right was a break in
the line of horses and vehicles. He spurred through. He
could hear Hogan shout something; the whoops of the
settlers followed him. Behind him, the pull of them was an
almost tangible drag.

He had not counted on the dust. It was so dense that he
knew they would not be able to follow him; he slowed
enough to let them bunch, so that one could follow the
other and the leaders could follow him. His black Stetson
pulled down, Cuff came up beside him, riding easily. Vern
glanced back. He saw a mass of riders and drawn faces.

Now that they were in the clear, he could think about
direction. On a map, the line they would follow would
take the curve of a drawn bow, with the bowstring on the
west. After the flat prairie, there would be rich
bottomlands—then gullies and brush—then another

wedge of prairie, and at last a wide, sandy wash with a clear stream winding over the sand. Beyond that, held in a turn of the broad stream called Pawnee Creek, was the townsite.

Ahead of him, a rider sprang from the saddle and began pounding a stake. Other men were already pounding stakes. The closer claims would go first, the accessible and less desirable ones. Lucky riders on fast horses would get the better claims. Riders who pushed their luck too far and met the mob coming down from Kansas would wind up in a scramble—a few claims and a swarm of takers.

Through the muted clatter of hoofs he heard a horse go down with a grunt. Glancing back, he saw that the rider was one of Hogan's men. The man skidded and sprawled and got up dazedly, looking for his horse. The animal lunged up but waited for him. He was tempted to wait for him to remount, but seeing the long and ragged line stretching in both directions, he turned and kept riding.

In three minutes the line had begun to thin out. Some had fallen behind, others had stopped to take claims. The last of the buggies and sulkies had been left behind. A few cavalrymen rode with the leaders. Vern began to bear northeast. They came to the first gully, a clean split in the prairie. The tops of a few small trees showed above it. He rode along the bank a few yards until he came to a slide, put his horse down it and sprinted across the sand to the far side of the arroyo. Topping out, he glanced back and saw the riders stringing across the wash, Cuff first, then some men he did not know, then Spence and Johnson. He held his horse in and let one of the settlers come up.

"There's some good land about a half-mile ahead. I'll wave my hat when we pass the marker."

The man passed the word back. Vern pulled out ahead. He wanted a lead on the others so that he could spot the marker without delay. Still running strongly, his horse surged ahead. He glanced east and west and saw with satisfaction that there was no rider ahead of him; the gully had slowed down the rest of them. In his mind he pictured the mile-corner he was looking for—a notched stone surveyor's monument near some big elm trees. A half-mile from it, in any direction of the compass, were half-mile marks. The land was dark and fertile, rolling but not rough.

He topped a little hill and looked down into a shallow valley in the bottom of which was the green scope of elms he was looking for. From a branch of one of those trees a branding-iron should be hanging—memento of a long-forgotten calf-roundup. A sense of guilt assailed him, that he should be party to the destruction of this range which had once been as free and beautiful as a hawk hovering on an updraft of air.

He heard the others coming up fast, and rode on down the slope. He looked for the monument—a low, rounded stone about fifty feet from one of the trees. Then he saw the grass hiding it, and rode toward it. He had a little shock of surprise: beside the stone marker fluttered a flag on a branch driven into the ground.

Three men rode from the trees with rifles across their saddles.

They stopped near the marker, and he looked at them. He had a swift expectation that one of them would be Trago. But he had never seen them before. Yet he recognized the breed: sooners. They might have been camped in those trees for a week! One of them, thin and sober, with dark, unshaven jaws, sat his horse in Farrell's path and shook his head, while the others moved in.

"Too late, brother," he said. "We've been here ten minutes. Look at the time on the flag."

"You're a liar. Your horses aren't lathered."

"Good horses don't lather." The sooner smiled. He made a subtly threatening motion with his rifle. Just then the first of the homesteaders came over the crest of the hill. The sooner began crowding in.

"Move along, brother," the tall man said.

Vern looked at them with a coal of wrath igniting in him. Tramps, adventurers, speculators: no stock in trade but bluff and greed. The land had been full of them on the last opening, and despite the cavalry they had infested it again.

"Well—" he said dubiously, and began turning his horse. Then he swerved it back into the sooner's horse and sank the spurs in. His horse squealed and reared, striking at the other horse. He drew his Colt and swung it at the rider's head. He hit him across the ear, stunning him. The man's rifle clattered down and his horse began to pitch. Vern drove at the next man and when he turned his rifle on him he fired. The shot hit the man in the arm. There were shouts from the other men riding up, and the third sooner whirled his horse and spurred into the trees. Settlers were all around now, staring at the men on the ground.

"Sooners," Farrell snapped. "They threw down on me. Whoever stays here had better disarm the one I slugged, and watch for the other. They've marked at least three of the corners for you. Look for the flags and put up your own."

The settlers hesitated a moment. Then one man jumped down. "Good enough for me!" He tore out the stake the sooners had erected and began pounding in his own.

Against the dry, scorching wind, they rode on.

They trailed across the low hills, dropping homesteaders by two's and three's. They seemed to have a fair lead. From time to time a rider would be seen on a rise to the east or west, flogging his horse along. The main body of the boomers was a minute or two behind. Gullies, hills, and islands of trees passed as though a finger were tracing the course across a map. In the heat-haze, Vern distinguished a dark line of trees. As it came closer, he knew what it meant.

He told the men nearest him, "Pawnee Creek! Best claims are just this side."

"What about the townsite?" the man panted. His face was red and streaked with sweat and dirt.

"Across the creek. Couple of miles."

Far away, a ghost-echo he could not be sure of having heard, a train-whistle floated on the wind. Due north, a Rock Island line ran along the Kansas border, dipping down into the Strip as it pushed West. A lot of men would be making the run on railroad cars—leaping out at each momentary stop to race on foot for claims. But there was no railroad near Pawnee—just a little cavalry camp and a few dozen soldiers, keepers of the peace.

The eager, dark earth spread from the base of a little range of hills all the way to the river. Even to a man who had never watched a plow turn up a polished curl of soil from down deep, the land looked good. It had been waiting since the ice-cap moved across it for men to make it work. It was strong earth and young earth, and the settlers' eyes shone when they saw it. Crossing it, he pointed out the mile corners. They could find the half-mile marks themselves.

Then the wind began to taste of trees and leaves, of bushes growing in wet soil. The horses were slowing, winded and leg-weary with the twenty-minute run. Some of the homesteaders began angling off to take their quarter-section share of the loamy earth.

Old Man Cuff looked back. "Man, here they come!" he exclaimed. "We'd better pour it on. Some of them must've thought we knew where we were going. They're sure following."

Down the hillsides poured a broken file of racing horsemèn. Already they were streaming across the bottomlands, where Hogan's men were beginning frantically to search for the markers and drive their stakes. Farrell estimated they had a quarter-mile lead.

CHAPTER 23

He had been alert for sooners ever since the first encounter. He had seen no evidence of any, however. But as he led what was left of the column, fifteen or eighteen men, up the trail into the trees, he saw a line of tracks leading toward the river. The tracks followed the old trail they themselves were on, a plain trail which had been used by Indians for centuries. Sooners usually traveled in multiples, but this rider had been alone.

Then he saw the flash of color in the thick green brush as they entered the grove of trees, and he knew it was neither a sooner nor a cavalryman. What he had seen was a horse tied in the growth a hundred feet below the trail. But it had not been well-hidden, nor was an apaloosa easy to hide, with its white coat and bold mottling of liver-colored spots. He knew instantly that it was Trago's horse. Trago—wound-sick or hurried, or else he would have hidden the horse better.

For a moment he held his horse back, searching for a

sign of the rancher. He thought of Trago's black eye behind the sights of a rifle, drawing a bead on him. In back of him horses were snorting, and Cuff panted:

"What's keepin' you? Them horses will pile up, boy!"

Leaning over the saddle-swell, Vern let the horse out.

A large root had grown across the trail; the pony jumped it and swerved on down to the wide and sandy bed of the stream. The stream-bed was about a hundred yards wide. Beyond it were more trees, and beyond the trees a smudge of woodsmoke against the sky. He knew by the smoke that they had come to the site of Pawnee. Thinking of Trago, his inclination was to keep the horse dodging as he crossed the creek. But Trago would have taken his shot by now. He was hiding; he was wounded; perhaps he was dead. But now the homesteaders were behind him, and it was too late for Trago to fire.

He came to the stream of clear warm water winding erratically over the sand. Spray flew as his horse hit the water. It was shallow, less than a foot deep, and it hardly slowed the horse as it lunged through. The cold spray exhilarated the riders; he could hear them whooping as they hit the water. Then he was on the dry sand again and cutting for the break in the trees beyond which was the flat land stretching for a mile or more. The horse lunged up a bank through the hot, redolent shade, and again the broad vista was before him.

He saw the troopers, first, deployed about an area of perhaps two hundred acres. At the left was the tent-city in which they had been camped. The prairie blossomed with little white flags on short stakes, the flags fluttering in the hot wind.

Suddenly he heard a distant whoop. Far north across the prairie he saw dust. From a dip in the earth he saw a line of horsemen ride into view and come sweeping toward the city of stakes. The Kansas settlers! He turned his head, hearing the others pounding up beside him, and bawled the news.

"Take your claims! We've got company!"

Spence and Johnson pressed in beside him, their faces

dirt-streaked. Vern grinned at them. Winded and sun-scorched, they looked exhausted. He swung his arm.

"Stay with me, now. The first claim I spot will be Johnson's. . . ."

It was impossible to tell what would be the business district of this metropolis-of-tomorrow, but a good guess might be the geographical center of it. He led out that way, as the settlers spread out across the prairie. Several of them dropped off within a few hundred feet and pounded their stakes. A trooper waved his hat as they went by.

"Take one fer me!" he yelled.

The lots were laid out four-square, with a stake at each southwest corner. Between each line of stakes was a wide strip of prairie which by tonight would be known as a street. The streets looked foolishly wide; yet when the buildings went up they would seem narrow. They loped across-lots until they seemed to be at the heart of the town. The Kansas riders were only a few blocks away, spreading over the north side of town. The Kansas riders were only a few blocks away, spreading over the north side of town like grasshoppers.

Farrell pulled up beside a stake. Johnson sprang down. They rode on to the next stake in line, and he yelled at Bill Spence: "She's all yours!"

When he spurred toward the next stake he saw a Kansan driving onto the lot from the north. He sprinted the horse, lying low over its withers, and made a sliding stop and dived for the government stake. He planted his own stake upright and the Kansas settler turned his horse sharply and went for a claim on the other side of the street.

Vern looked back down the street. Spence's horse was standing with its head hanging. The little cowboy loosened the cinch, dropped on the ground and lay back to rest, looking like a dead man. Farther along, Johnson had pounded his stake and was sitting on the ground beside it.

Pawnee was full of men and horses. Two men were having a fist-fight a hundred feet away, and a trooper rode

upon them with his saber laid back over his shoulder.
Other men were running across-lots looking for better
claims than they had already taken.

Within ten minutes there was at least one man on every
lot in town. Gazing over the town, Vern was reminded of
an army exercise—a man and a horse every few
rods—waiting for a signal. Under the hot sun he looked at
Pawnee for a long time. He could almost see the
metropolis it was going to be. Dream-like, the town grew
in his mind. It had buildings and vacant lots—young trees
and small homes—churches and livery stables. Hammers
rang as new buildings went up. People would be living in
this town tonight; within a month they would be holding
meetings to decide on a mayor and town council, and
someone would suggest that it was not too early to think
about sidewalks. Close to a creek and a railroad, with
other railroads coming in, Pawnee could not fail to
prosper. It was a youngster with all the advantages.

He lay on his back with his hat over his face. The rays
of the sun flailed at him; the heat of the earth baked him
from beneath. But it was good to rest for a few minutes,
and while he rested his thoughts went back to Tom Trago.

Dead or wounded? If he was dead, the horse should be
unsaddled and Trago's body laid away. If he was
wounded, he should be tended. He should be jailed,
too—but for what? No one could say he had set fire to
those tents in Hogan. Perhaps no one could prove he had
lynched Dick Sullivan, now that Earl Slade was dead.
Trago, perhaps, was as free as anyone in Oklahoma.

A warmth of anger crept over him.

He had the slyness of the Indians and the predatory
animals he had warred against all his life. He could kill,
burn and get away with it. But it would be ironic if the
man he had saved from lynching turned on him and had
him jailed for assault and attempted murder!

He sat up, dazed with the heat, feeling a trifle sick at his
stomach. His face felt dry and flushed. He took his Colt
out and looked over the loads. His head clearing, he rode

back to Spence. Spence, who had moved over into the shade of his horse, sat up.

"Man, oh, man! That was a ride!"

"Baked all the meanness out of you, I reckon. I'm going down and water my horse," Vern told him. "Keep an eye on my claim while I'm gone. Then I'll come back and spell you while you go."

"Okay."

He rode back to the river crossing and left his horse tied in the shade on the near side. He had seen Trago's horse below the crossing on the far side. He walked down the creek a hundred yards. If there was any chance to surprise Trago, assuming he was alive, he intended to take it. Trago's attention would be on the crossing.

He walked across the sand to the shallow stream winding down the broad watercourse. The water soaked his boots luxuriously as he stepped into it, rose above them after a few strides and spilled over into the tops. The coolness went all through him. The hard gravel bed crunched under his feet. He waded the stream quietly. Once he stooped to scoop up a handful of water to slake his thirst. Some more settlers arrived on exhausted ponies and came lunging across the creek-bed toward Pawnee.

Then he saw the horse standing in the wild-plum tangles against the far bank.

Suddenly he was afraid, shaken by the cold second thoughts of a soldier going into battle. He drew his gun and walked quietly across the sand toward the horse. He thought, *I can go back. He's not my responsibility*. But that was the trouble: Trago *was* his responsibility. It would be weeks before there would be any law in the Strip. If he recovered from the wound, which might be slight, he would not leave Oklahoma until he had gotten square with the settlers he hated.

He thought these things, and kept walking. Gnats swam in his vision like spots before his eyes. In the stream-bed it was suffocatingly hot. He could feel a trickle of perspiration sliding down his chest. He wiped his hand on his trouser-leg.

He pushed through the dense, molasses-smelling brush until he stood at the edge of a patch of bare ground on which the horse stood. The horse stood with its reins dangling, turning its head to regard him. He held his breath and gazed around. Suddenly he saw Trago lying face-down at the lower end of the clearing. There was blood on his clothing—an adobe-colored stain saturating his trousers.

He went toward him cautiously. The rancher's arm was crumpled under him; his face was turned away. He appeared to have bled a lot. There were marks in the earth as though he had crawled here from where the horse was standing, trying to reach the water. He could not tell whether he was dead or dying, and at last he holstered the Colt and knelt to roll him onto his back.

Trago scuttled away, pulling his gun from beneath him.

He scarcely recognized the drawn, yellow features. Trago's mustache looked abnormally black against his sallow face. His eyes were black too, but without luster. The lines and pockets of his face had been deepened by pain and loss of blood. His lips looked dry and stiff; they separated with difficulty as he spoke, lying there on his side.

"Back up, boy. Back up."

Vern slowly rose and took a step back.

"Drop your gun," the rancher said. Vern unbuckled his gunbelt and let the harness drop to the sand. "That's good. Now—get out your knife."

"What for? That bullet's deep. I can't cut it out of you."

"It ain't deep," Trago said. "Let's see that knife."

Groping for his pocket-knife, Vern told him: "It must be deep, amount you've bled."

Trago put his hand over the big, dried stain on his hip. "It *was* deep. It's worked near the surface. I packed the hole with a piece of my shirt-tail and stopped the bleeding."

Vern snapped the sharp blade out. "Do I drop it, or hand it to you?"

Trago unbuckled his belt and pulled his trousers and drawers down to his hip. There was a mass of dried blood a couple of inches below his hip-bone, with a sheen of fresh blood on the wad of rag he had stuffed into the hole.

"You're gonna do it," he said. "I'd 'a' had a try at it myself, if I hadn't lost my knife. But I reckon you can operate just as well as me, and I'll kind of assist you." He waved the Colt wearily. "Let's go, Congressman."

"What's to keep me from putting this in your liver, Tom? I'd just as soon, and that's the truth."

Trago gave him a yellow grin. "A Colt always outranks a knife, I've heard. Come on. I ain't got forever."

"Forever's all you have got, without a doctor. You'll bleed to death."

"There's a doctor right here, and if he don't go to cuttin' mighty quick—"

Vern knelt again. "Be a pleasure, Tom, if that's how you want it. Where's the slug?"

Trago touched the blue lump under the flesh. It was on the side of his hip, so that it was no trick to cover Farrell with the gun while he bent over him. Vern touched the lump and felt the ragged bulk of the forty-five-caliber slug. He tested the knife-blade with his thumb, then looked at the Colt.

"As a favor to me—will you uncock that? When I start cutting, you're going to flinch."

"I'm steady as a rock. Try me."

Vern sighed. He plunged the knife into the damp sand to clean it, wiped it on his trousers, and laid his free hand on Trago's hip. With thumb and forefinger, he stretched the flesh across the bullet, making it stand up clearly. He could see Trago's hand shaking.

"Steady now—"

He laid the blade on the flesh, waiting a moment for Trago to get himself in hand. Then he made a small slice. Trago's breath hissed in through his teeth.

"God damn you!" he groaned.

"I told you you ought to have a doctor."

"Go on! God damn you!"

Vern cut down to the bullet, while Trago lay still and bitterly cursed him. He extended the cut until he thought he could pop the slug out, but the lead had struck bone and taken hooklike edges. With half his attention on the Colt, he enlarged the cut until he could work the bullet out. Trago sensed it at once, taking in a long breath.

"Is it out?"

Vern showed it to him. Trago took it in his free hand and hurled it into the bushes. "You know where I got that?"

"Sure. But you forced my hand."

"Get my horse."

Vern walked to the pony and picked up the reins. Truning back, he saw that Trago was on his feet, tucking in his shirt-tail. The Colt was still in his hand. Vern wet his lips. There was not much time left, and he knew what Trago would do as soon as he was in the saddle and sure of himself. He made a quick calculation. With luck, he could swing the horse, get into the saddle and get out of range. But Trago would probably shoot the horse, and that story would be over quickly.

"Bring it here!" Trago ordered.

He seemed to have forgotten the knife with which Vern had cut out the bullet. It was still in his hand. He moved it so that the point rested on his middle finger and the haft was concealed in his sleeve. By letting the blade slip downward through his fingers, he could arm himself quickly. He led the horse back, the reins in his left hand. Trago, yellow-sick, his eyes glazed, took the reins and stepped back one pace.

"You know what I'm going to do, don't you?"

"I could guess."

"I'd be a damned fool to leave somebody behind who knew I was in trouble, wouldn't I? Somebody that killed the only man who'd have ridden with me?"

"What did you expect?" Vern said. "He fired at me."

"You had your chance to ride with me. But you were too smart. Smart young farmer-lover. I pulled you out of jail, and that was how you thanked me."

He worked the horse around and put a foot in the

stirrup, keeping Vern under the eye of the Colt. As he swung up, Vern let the knife drop into his hand. Then he flung it up in a powerful underhand throw. Point-first, it smacked into Trago's midriff just below the ribs. With a soft thud, it buried itself to the haft. Trago's face contorted with shock. He had just been seating himself in the saddle when the knife went home, and he continued to get set for an instant, easing his hip painfully for the ride. Then pain washed through his face, and he stretched himself high in the saddle.

Vern dodged behind the pony. Trago twisted and tried to level the Colt. The staggering report of a shot made the leaves tremble. Trago's horse shied into the brush. Vern was on the other side of the horse now, reaching up to seize Trago's gun-arm. He caught his wrist and dragged him sidewise from the saddle. The rancher landed heavily on his side with a muffled groan. Vern saw the Colt lying in the sand a few feet away, and he picked it up, cocked it, and stepped away.

Trago rolled over on his back. One leg drew up slowly. The knife protruded grimly from his body like an unnatural growth. His lips pulled away from the yellow teeth and his face gradually assumed the gaunt, grinning expression of a death-mask. Vern stepped in and drew the knife out. He looked at it, and then threw it in the brush.

He waited there until he was sure Trago was dead. It did not seem proper, somehow, to leave before the play was ended, for Trago was not just a man dying, a man gone bad like a rogue bull: Trago was the last of a breed, the no-quarter Indian fighter who did not try to tame the big, free land which gave him his living, but was content to fight it on its own terms.

Trago's fingers slowly opened. There was a crashing of brush up the river, and Vern glanced that way and saw some homesteaders lunging through the thickets into the wash. They flogged their tired horses across the sand toward Pawnee. He looked back at Tom Trago, whose eyes were beginning to dull.

Trago and the Cherokee Strip were dead.

• • •

He stayed at Pawnee until dark. Supper fires began to blaze about the prairie. Tents had gone up and a few wagons had arrived from north and south. Farrell had reported the killing to the cavalry commander, and now Trago's body lay under a tarp in a tent, awaiting burial.

Spence and Johnson stayed at the claims. In the big, dark night, Vern started back to town. On a far ridge, a prairie wolf howled. Though as a cattleman he had fought wolves all his life, there was something sad in the sound, in knowing that soon their kind would be gone forever from this country. But, he thought, so will I—gone to a range where the cattle trade was king, and a man with spurs stood a little higher than he stood anywhere else.